TEN SHORT STORIES
FOR THE 2018
RYEDALE BOOK FESTIVAL

For Paul - see my story - You will probably smile!

Dad

RYEDALE
BOOK FESTIVAL

BLACKTHORN PRESS

Blackthorn Press, Blackthorn House
Middleton Rd, Pickering YO18 8AL
United Kingdom

www.blackthornpress.com

ISBN 978 1 906259 50 1

2018

FOREWORD

We are delighted to have worked with Blackthorn Press on this short story competition. The response to the competition was phenomenal this year. Congratulations to all the writers whose stories were selected for this impressive shortlist of ten.

As a festival, we are committed to promoting the enjoyment of reading to all ages and are proud to introduce new and emerging writers to our audience. An important part of our work is encouraging anyone to have a go at writing creatively and entering a short story competition is a good way to for people to begin and develop their writing careers.

Selecting a shortlist from the applicants was a challenge for the judges, who all commented on the high standard of work submitted. I would like to thank Alan Avery, Libby Pearson and Ana Richards for agreeing to take on this remit and also for their time and commitment to the competition. I am sure they did not realise the magnitude of the task ahead when they volunteered to take part!

Special thanks go to Blackthorn Press for producing this book and for initiating a short story competition that encourages writers and enables new talent to be discovered.

I am confident that you will thoroughly enjoy and appreciate the diversity of the top ten short stories that are collected together into this anthology.

Sarah Tyson
Festival Director

RYEDALE BOOK FESTIVAL

The Ryedale Book Festival was established in 2012 by readers in the Ryedale community. It is a charitable organisation whose objective is to promote a love of reading, storytelling and creative writing.

It organises an interesting programme of high quality events that take place throughout the year at various locations across the rural district.

Dedicated volunteers work hard to ensure their guest artists are warmly welcomed and their audiences enjoy the opportunity to engage with imaginative literary activities in the annual programme.

The Festival Team is extremely grateful to everyone, both in the Ryedale community and publishing world, who supports its endeavours for readers and writers to celebrate and share their love for books and the spoken word in beautiful Ryedale.

www.ryedalebookfestival.com

CONTENTS

Notes on the Authors

PATRICK BELSHAW

Patrick Belshaw lives in Richmond, North Yorkshire. He is a former H.M. Inspector of Schools and holds a PhD from Newcastle University. He is a widower with three sons and three grandsons. An established author with over a dozen short stories in print, he says of his work that he writes largely for his own enjoyment and also because he feels oddly compelled to.

TOM BRYAN

Tom Bryan was born in Winnipeg, Canada in 1950, but has been long resident in Scotland, his mother's country. He is a widely published and broadcast poet, fiction and non-fiction writer and editor of literary magazines. He was the founder of "The Eildon Tree" magazine, still going in the Scottish Borders. Tom plays a bit of harmonica and writes dramatic pieces which have been performed as far away as Tula, in Russia.

ALAN BRYANT

Alan Bryant lives in Mumbles, in a small house with 'sea glimpses' conveniently placed near the bus stop, the chip shop and the castle he looks up at in awe every day. Since retiring he is delighted to have time to write again and has gained a BA in Creative Writing and Literature with the Open University. He is a published short story writer and is working on a crime novel.

PAUL B. COHEN

Paul B. Cohen read English at Leeds University and studied further in the U.S.A. Formerly a freelance theatre and film reviewer, his plays have been seen in various cities in the United States. His short stories have appeared in a number of journals. His tale 'Lecha Dodi' won first place in Moment magazine's 2014 Short Fiction Awards. He is currently writing novels.

AOIFE INMAN

Aoife Inman is a historian, artist and general lover of words both spoken and typed. Based in Manchester, she sent her first eight-page story off to a publishing house at the age of 12, complete with a handwritten note, kickstarting a life-long obsession with writing. She is a member of the 'Writing Squad' and has a long list of writing credits including being long-listed for the 2016 Royal Academy Short Story Award.

BARBARA MURRAY

Barbara and her Spanish husband Paco divide their time between Barcelona and their home in the Yorkshire Dales. Cumbrian author Barbara was inspired to become a writer through working with the multi-generational stories and dramas of her family business clients. Barbara enjoys uncovering lessons from people's lives and historical events and blending these into contemporary stories about family and community dynamics.

JOANNE PRESTON

Joanne Preston was born and raised in Scarborough, North Yorkshire. She fell in love with story-telling at a young age, and has a degree in English with Educational Studies from the University of Hull. She lives in Bolton, Greater Manchester, with her husband and young daughter. This is her first published work.

STEPHEN EDWARD REID

Stephen Edward Reid graduated from Bolton University with a degree in Film/TV and Writing. He has written and directed a number of plays and short films and one of his feature length screenplays is currently in development. He now lives in York with his family and is working on his first novel.

STEPHEN WADE

Stephen Wade was born in Leeds. His main career has been as a teacher and lecturer, but he now writes full-time. He has a special interest in the history of crime and law, and he has written widely on cases from all parts of Yorkshire. His short stories have been in a number of magazines and anthologies, and his favourite themes and subjects tend to be humorous. *We All Fall in Love in Amnesia, Nebraska* is a story in a developing collection of tales set in the American Mid-West.

GLENDA YOUNG

Glenda Young became a freelance writer in 2015. She contributes to a variety of magazines, including 'The People's Friend', the longest running women's magazine in the world. An avid fan and writer about 'Coronation Street', she writes her own weekly 'soap', *Riverside*, for 'The People's Friend'. Her debut novel, 'Belle of the Back Streets' will be published this year.

FOLLOWING BALLOONS

Patrick Belshaw

Such a nice man. Maybe I was worrying for nothing?

The school had set up the meeting. Concerned about my friends, they said. I couldn't understand it. I didn't have any friends. Not that kind, anyway. That was the problem, they said. Not for me, I said. I was quite happy as I was.

It was my Dad who took me, of course. My Mam's an actress. Not famous, or anything. You won't have heard of her. Works at some theatre. In Leeds, I think. Small parts, mainly. But while she's working in one play, she's often rehearsing for the next – so she's always either acting or rehearsing. Never has the time to take me anywhere. It's always down to my Dad. He's a musician: a bassoonist. Teaches part-time. Goes from school to school. "Very pathetic," he tells people, and then he laughs as if it's all a big joke. I don't get it.

My Dad often says things I don't get. Take this man we went to see. I heard my Dad say he was a trick cyclist – which I know can't be right, because you should have seen the size of him! Huge, he was. At least, the top half of him was. Large, round head. Big fat belly, stretching his belt. I thought he would burst his trousers! But he had these short, spindly legs. He looked so top heavy, it made me laugh. I couldn't see *him* riding a bike. He'd always be falling off! Perhaps that was his trick – staying on? Nice man, though. Henderson, I think he was called. Very smiley face. Not quite sure who he was. Not a doctor, I don't think. No white coat. And nothing round his neck for listening to chests with. Seemed very interested in

1

Mam for some reason. Could he have seen her on the stage, I wondered?

"Now, tell me about your little friends," he said, once he got going. "Why so many? What is it about them that attracts you?"

"Well," I told him, "I like the shape of them. I like their big, round faces. Faces you can trust. Like moons, they are. Especially those that float near the ceiling. I can look up, and there they are – my very own full moons. And they're so smooth and soft. I often reach out and stroke them. Those I keep tied close to the floor, I mean. I like the smell of them, as well." I paused. I had to be careful. I could feel myself starting to bubble over. It always happened when I was asked to talk about my friends. It wouldn't do to get over-excited. Not everyone understood. The nice man seemed to understand, though. He was smiling all over his own round face, encouraging me to go on. "And one of the nicest things about them is that they're there – all around me – but they're quiet. They don't speak till they're spoken to. I like that."

"So they *can* speak, then?" I sensed he was getting excited now.

"Oh, yes – when I want them to. I can get them to talk."

"And how do you do that?"

"Simple," I said. "I draw my fingers across their skin and sort of pinch them. That soon sets them off. That soon gets their squeaky voices going."

"And you can understand what they're saying?"

"Of course," I said. Was he stupid, or something? "Be no point if I couldn't, would there?"

"Of course not." The nice man's face grew even smilier. "Thank you, Kelvin – that's very interesting." He looked down

2

at some notes on his slippery knee. "And how many of these little friends have you got, may I ask?"

"Scores," my Dad answered. I wondered how long it would be before he chipped in. A broad grin filled the space between his bassoon-blowing cheeks. "Hundreds of them, all floating about. Like clouds. Yes – head forever in the clouds, my boy. That right, Kelvin?" I nodded. "Yes – all over the house, they are. In every room. But mainly in his bedroom. You should see them in there. All bobbing about. You can't get stirred for them. Not that we mind. It's his room. Other rooms, though – that's a different matter. The kitchen, for example. Wouldn't do to have them in there, now would it? Not the helium ones, anyway." He paused to laugh at his little joke. I'd heard it before. "Yes – we've got hundreds. Different sizes, different colours, different materials. Singles, doubles, clusters. Balloon mad, he is. Always has been, ever since he was a small child – well, a baby, really."

"Really?" The nice man was getting excited again. "Since he was a baby? Now that *is* interesting. Can you remember when it all started?"

"I can actually," my Dad said. "The very day, in fact. Twelfth Night, it was. I was taking down the decorations. Broke off to read him his bedtime story. I thought he'd gone to sleep – even before I'd finished – but he must've crept downstairs to the sitting room, the little monkey, and smuggled them upstairs. He'd only be about eighteen months at the time – and there he was, lying fast asleep, his head resting between two white balloons. They'd gone down a bit by then – but even so, they could have burst. He'd have got a nasty shock then, eh? And bits of rubber lying about? He might've choked on those."

3

"Yes, I can still remember those balloons," I said. "The feel of them – so warm and soft and smooth against my lips. They were lovely, those two."

"Your mother didn't think so!" my Dad said. "She was cross – cross with the pair of us – when she heard about it."

"She wasn't there, then?" Mr. Smiley asked.

"No, she was at the theatre. Doing *Twelfth Night,* as a matter of fact." Dad laughed. "She was hardly ever in at evening time. We were used to that, weren't we, Kelvin?"

"Yes – but it was lovely when she *was* at home," I said.

"I'm sure," said Mr. Smiley. "Love your mother, do you, Kelvin?"

"I'll say!" I cried. "She's lovely. No, not just lovely – beautiful! Everybody says so. She's an actress, you know."

"Yes, so your father tells me." Mr. Smiley nodded, and his eyes twinkled. "Miss her, do you?"

"Yes. Or I used to, when I was little. Missed her a lot, then. Especially at bedtimes. Dad's great. Tells really good stories. But he smells of whisky and fags." I looked across at him and gave him a big smile "and he's very hairy! Mam was never hairy, of course." The thought of a hairy Mam suddenly made me laugh. "No – always soft and smooth, she was. And when she leaned over to kiss me goodnight, she always smelled nice."

"I can imagine," said Mr. Smiley, beaming at me. Then he turned to my Dad. "Well – all those balloons! I'm trying to imagine. Perhaps I could see for myself?"

And he did see for himself. He came two Saturdays later, in the afternoon. A 'home visit', he called it. My Mam couldn't be there, of course. Doing a matinee. Mr. Nice-and-Smiley

4

seemed disappointed, I could tell. Perhaps he had once seen her on stage? Perhaps he was a fan? But when he saw my collection, he soon looked smiley again. His eyes opened wide with amazement. Wide and round and shiny. A bit like my balloons.

"Wow!" he said, bobbing underneath them.

"So many!" he said, weaving in and out of them.

"Wonderful!" he cried, as he lost himself in the jungle of them.

"And not just balloons..." He was admiring my things on the wall. Pictures, mostly. Hot-air balloons, and the men who invented them. But other bits and pieces, as well. For instance, I had a saucer decorated with red, white and blue balloons. Bought it in a shop in Kirkbymoorside. Bought a fan in there as well – you know, one of those things you waft about, to cool yourself with? – with a man holding a string of balloons painted on it. Mr. Smiley seemed very interested in my pictures. Going back to them, he pointed at one and gave me one of his big smiles. "Ah, Montgolfier – yes?"

"Yes – but which one?" I knew I had him there. "There were two of them, you see. They were brothers. Joseph-Michel and Jacques-Etienne. That one is Etienne. Everybody seems to remember their last name. And everybody says, 'Yes – the first hot air balloon.' But they're wrong. It was only the first to carry people. The very first was launched by a man called Pilatre De Rozier. It stayed in the air for fifteen minutes – and it carried a sheep, a duck and a rooster! Bet you didn't know that?"

"You bet right," laughed Mr. Smiley. He turned and stepped closer to my Dad. He dropped his voice, but I could still catch what he was saying. "Very impressive. Your boy knows his stuff. But all this ballonabilia! I mean, we all like balloons, I guess. No harm in that. We tend to associate them with parties, don't we? And therefore with play, with gaiety, with frivolity. But this?" He swept his arm sideways and several balloons bobbed up and down, caught in the draught. "This is something else. Serious stuff. I've never observed anything quite like it. Not just a collector, our Kelvin, is he? Knows the science – the maths, the physics. Knows the history. Knows his subject inside-out."

"You could say that!" Dad laughed. "Never puts his mind to anything else. That's why they're concerned about him at school. But one thing leads to another, that's what I say. I'm not worried. Far from it. He's a bright boy. I think he'll go far." He paused and gave me a smile. "Oh, I know what people think. And yes, it must seem a bit weird. But no harm in that, eh? Chip off the old block, in that respect." He laughed. "I mean, look at me. Spend hours and hours every week with a great big pipe in my mouth – and never an ounce of baccy in it!" He laughed again. "Yes, bassoonists, balloonists – all a little crazy. A bit balloonery, a bit bassoonery, a bit buffoonery, the lot of them!"

That was my Dad all over. Always using big, long words. Loved them, he did. Loved the sound of them, he said. 'Like music,' he would say. I reckon he made them up, most of them. Good at making things up, my Dad. I wish he hadn't said that, though. You know – used the 'crazy' word? He used it a lot when I was little. Something like it, anyway. "You're daft, me duck, you follow balloons; you wear your father's pantaloons!" – that's what he used to say. In a sing-song sort of voice. I didn't mind it much when I was little. In fact, it made me laugh. He was always coming out with funny little rhymes. Just trying to make me laugh, really. He meant no harm. But balloons aren't daft. They're fun. And people explore in them. Take them up high – much higher than Mount Everest. And they go round the world in them. They even race in them. Balloons are used in science, as well. They can tell things about the weather. So I hate that rhyme now. When I was little, my Mam used to say, "Call back to him. Tell him – you're the one who's daft, me duck; you're the one who follows bassoons!" But I never did.

When Mr. Smiley left, I went back to my room. My Dad saw him back to his car. My window was open a little bit. Not too much – draughts make my balloons go giddy: throw their strings into a right tangle! – but it was open enough for me to hear them talking on the drive. Words drifted up to me. Like gas-filled balloons. Nice balloon-words, some of them. But some were words I didn't want to hear.

impressive …. that workshop! …. amazing …. privilege to see it ….. those model hot-air balloons ….. quite a flotilla ….. built to scale, you say? – and they actually work? ….. he can make them fly? ….. yes. phenomenal – but worrying ….. not just a harmless bit of balloonmania ….. we're talking obsession here ….. serious already ….. could become dangerous if not treated ….. such a nice boy ….. don't want to see him in an institution, do we? ….. another session, yes ….. thorough examination ….. get your wife to come if she can ….. she could be the key ….. next Thursday all right – at three?

He was wrong there! I don't know what he meant by 'the key' – but whatever it was, my Mam couldn't be it. She couldn't be anything – for the simple reason that she's dead! I've been lying about her. Not the actress bit. You can check

7

that out. But she died when I was three. Suicide, they said. We were living in Canada then. Found in the river, she was, with reeds in her mouth and stones in her pockets. Like Ophelia, Dad said – but I didn't get what he meant. Mam would've got it, he said. I didn't get that, either. Not long after she died, we came to England.

We often pretended she was still alive, Dad and me. I don't know why. It helped, though – you know, in the early days, when I knew she wasn't coming home from rehearsals? Dad started it. It made things easier, he said. It helped to pretend. But pretending wasn't going to help me now. I thought at first that Mr. Smiley was on my side. Now I wasn't so sure. An *institution*, he said. I'm not daft. I know what that means. Big place, with lots of rooms. Like a prison. And me, all alone. None of my friends to keep me company. I couldn't bear that. *Next Thursday*, he said. So I hadn't got long. But a plan was already forming in my mind. Yes, I knew what I had to do. It was dangerous, but it was better than being locked up in a home somewhere.

I had done it before. Well, Dad and me had. When Pythagoras died. Pythagoras was our cat. Well, not really ours. He was a stray; we adopted him. Strange animal, he was, with eyes that didn't match and a broken tail that looked like a bent elbow. Funny name. Dad gave it to him. Anyway, when he died we strapped him into his basket, tied two helium balloons at each end of it, and let him float off high into the sky till he disappeared. It was a great send-off. His *Ascension*, Dad called it, as we watched him going slowly upwards towards the clouds. Then Dad laughed like a drain, saying that somebody, somewhere, was in for a bit of a shock when

Pythagoras came down to earth again and made his *Second Coming!* He said some funny things, my Dad.

Pythagoras was skinny. Four balloons were quite enough to see him off. I would need more. Lots more. I tried to work it out. I was a good eight times his weight, so I'd probably need about thirty-five. Maybe half-a-dozen really big ones. Six-footers. I'd have to buy those; and some more helium. There's this shop I go to, when we go into York. I could sneak off there one day. The rest of the cluster could be all different sizes. I'd need some of the smaller ones to burst if I was going too high – and to get ready for landing, of course – and some bottles of water for ballast, to throw overboard if I wasn't going high enough. I'd need some sort of harness, as well. But one of our folding deckchairs would do, I thought. I could strap myself into that.

Planning all this, I got really excited. What an adventure! I always said I would try cluster ballooning when I was bigger – and here I was, a bit earlier than I thought, making my dream come true. Well, maybe ... with a bit of luck! Taking after one of my heroes, as well. 'Lawnchair Larry'. That was his nickname. He was an American. Went up to 16,000 feet, using forty-five weather balloons fastened to his garden chair. How brave was that? Once I got up there, perhaps I could drift across to America and visit Larry? If he's still alive, that is. Need to catch the right winds, though. You can't steer clusters, you see. All you can do is find a good wind. They're big on cluster ballooning in America. I could learn a lot there. Maybe make a name for myself? Become a famous balloonist? Then I'd get back to England. Back to Dad. Dad'll be all right, mind. You know – while I'm away? He's got his fags and his booze – and his music, of course. He'll be happy bassooning while I'm happy ballooning. Hey – that sounds like him talking!

I launched my cluster while Dad was rehearsing with the Theatre Royal orchestra. He had no idea what was going on. Nothing unusual in that. I could do anything I liked. He would have no idea that I had nicked his holiday money to pay for the extra kit. Well – not for ages, he wouldn't. I think he forgets he's got it. Doesn't really need it, you see. We have plenty of money. My Mam left us lots. Got it from her Mam, I think. No, Dad just likes the idea of saving up – so every time he gets paid for a private lesson, he puts the money into a big jar. I often dip into it to buy stuff. I think he knows really – but he never says anything. I don't think he cares. And what does it matter, anyway? We never go on holiday. We never go anywhere. Too busy, both of us, doing what we like best. I've never cleaned him out before, mind. Not to worry: I'll pay him back one day. When I'm rich and famous.

"Goodbye, garden!" I cried, as my balloons sailed upwards. I was left dancing about in my chair below the bunches of strings. The speed took me by surprise. Good job the strapping was strong. "Goodbye, House! Goodbye, Lane! Goodbye, Steeple!" and, in less than a minute or two "Goodbye, Malton! Goodbye, Everywhere!"

High above a patchwork of fields, I was now being dragged towards the base of a long cloud. It was shaped like a cigar. Or, yes – like a zeppelin! I knew all about zeppelins. The first one, made by Count von Zeppelin, was very like a huge balloon. It seemed like a good sign. But it was cold and gloomy inside my cloudy zeppelin. Thank goodness I wasn't in it long.

10

Just long enough to make me glad I was wearing my balaclava helmet and my extra pair of trousers.

Above the cloud, I found myself caught in a fast stream of air. I was now travelling more sideways than upwards. But which way? Which way was America? And would my good friends, the balloons, keep me up? Just as worrying – would I be up here for ever? Because I'd heard Dad say: "Good friends, real friends, never let you down." So many questions. Questions with no answers. But for the moment I was alive – really alive! I felt so excited. What an adventure! I was free – free to follow my balloons. And supposing I never came down – or supposing I hurtled down too fast! – well, it was better than being locked away in an institution.

"Don't worry, Dad," I shouted down – down to a ground I couldn't see. "I'll be back. Till then, be happy for me. Thanks for believing in me."

He did believe in me, my Dad. Always said I would go far! Though how far I'm going, and where, I have no idea. Perhaps I'm just going there and back, to see how far it is? That was another one of his little jokes. Maybe it's not such a bad idea. I'll settle for it. I have little choice.

Yes, I was learning, when you follow balloons you have little choice.

FROM WHERE THERE ARE GHOST BEARS

Tom Bryan

"Ghost bears," they sneered. "How can *bears* be *ghosts*?"

I had said: "I come from a part of Canada with ghost bears. Ghost bears are black bears that are born white. *White* black bears. Our native peoples called them *ghost* bears."

But I had at least one friend in the class.

She said: "Well, our Kentucky is called the 'Blue Grass State' so I suppose if green grass can be blue, then black bears can be white."

"Phew!"

I hadn't seen any blue grass by then and wondered: if the grass is blue, maybe the sky is green? Stranger things were happening. There were eight of us in the house: my mum, her aunt and uncle and five children: 4 boys (my two brothers and two cousins) and one girl (me). We all came from northern places where there were no trees. My great aunt was from Orkney. She told me there was a millionaire behind every tree in Orkney. Then she laughed at her private joke. I understood nearly forty years later when I saw the barren moors and cliffs of her native island for the first time.

Front porch, living room, dining room, kitchen, back door, wooden porch of three steps. Back yard. What was that tree? Magic. Huge white flowers as big as dinner plates. It was a Flowering Dogwood. I asked about the tree and they said it was because its bark was used to treat dog mange or diseases of dog fur. My aunt also said its red berries were not for eating. "Leave them for the birds" she said and we did. If trees held magic, this one would.

It became my personal tree. It was in the far corner of the back yard and marked the limits of my child's world. My mum sometimes sat under the tree with me; my aunt did too. Neither my uncle nor any of the boys showed any interest in the tree but for me, that was a good thing.

I could see under the tree and think of the whispered words I had been hearing for many months. Death. Cancer. Chemotherapy. Adoption. My great-aunt could take all three of us if mum died and nobody else could. Yet, there was hope. I saw my mother's thin hair growing back and it looked bonny against the huge white flowers.

At first, until this strange world became more familiar, I needed something that was my own; the Dogwood was it.

Most of what was so new was also good, at first.

My great aunt found a small robin fallen from its nest, not yet fledged. Although she was busy with work in and out the home she put the small scrawny bird into a shoe box coated with cotton. She told me later she expected the bird to die overnight; it didn't. She fed it by eye dropper with warm milk and oatmeal. The bird grew until it was time to release it. Our whole family stood on the back porch as the tiny bird, still speckled, flew to the Dogwood and perched there. When we looked the next day, it was gone. It was gone for days or weeks or months, until one day in late autumn I was playing in the back yard. Looking above me on a Dogwood branch sat a robin. I quickly dug some worms from the side garden and the bird hopped to my arm and ate the worms. Nobody believed the story but it was true. We never saw the robin again.

Just slightly beyond the tree was a grassy alley which ran west until it came to a street far out of view. Good things came from there and I liked to think of the Dogwood as a gate which opened only to good things.

The girl who came to see me. Linda. She was dark. I am fair, blue eyed, red haired, just like my mum. Linda's hair was as brown as chocolate. I liked her eyes, so dark they were black. She came often and we sat under the shady tree. She was my first friend. Her name had lots of *a/ e/ i /o* in it. *Italy* she said, where her father came from. "What is this strange tree?" she asked. I told her. "It is a strange name for such a lovely flower. It should be more butterfly than dog." She smiled when I said it should have a nice-sounding name like her own name: *Bocatelli.*

The car from another time. My mum knew a woman named Sandy. Sandy and her husband had a Model T Ford. One summer night it came down the alley, beyond the Dogwood. The evening sun shone on its polished metal. The car looked like a moving rainbow. It stopped near the tree and one by one, we were given a ride down the main streets. Everybody looked and waved.

Fireflies/lightning bugs. I had never seen them before but one summer night the backyard tinkled with their lights and many adorned the Dogwood. *This southern land is full of wonders* I said to my mum who smiled, although she did not smile so often in those days.

Cicadas. I was frightened when I first heard them. The rising chorus, like rushing water, then tailing off. I found a cicada on the base of the dogwood. As big as my finger, shiny green and metallic, looking like a small tank. They lived underground for years then came into the daylight to sing at dusk.

14

But next, a series of things emerged from the Dogwood and beyond that made me take my decision, one that plunged our family of eight into panic and changed our lives.

I will try list those things in order, that came from the grass and trees, from the green alley beyond, and from the flowering tree itself.

Clancy and the starlings. Clancy was an old man who lived just within the view from our back yard. At dusk, thousands of starlings would gather in the maple tree in front of his house. Clancy stood under the tree. He had a double barrelled shotgun. He fired twice and the dead starlings would rain down upon him. He then raked up the dead starlings and burned them in an oil drum in his garden. I had nightmares about purple starlings, raining like ripe plums from the sky.

Sheila's Snapping Turtle. Sheila was older than me. One day, Sheila had a huge snapping turtle. "Good eating" she said. "Come see this" she said. Her brother took a broomstick and goaded the snapper. It bit on the stick, stretching its neck, which her brother then cut off with a Boy Scout axe. I think Sheila's family ate the snapping turtle meat later. They varnished its shell and nailed it to a maple tree in their back yard. In my dreams, the starlings are now falling at the base of the varnished shell, ravaged by huge snapping turtles – all underneath our Dogwood blossoms.

Ginger Morgan. She appeared one day from beyond our back yard. "You bitch" she screamed. She began to hit me with a huge strip of bamboo. I was wearing shorts and my legs were bare. Huge welts rose from her beating. Perhaps she was beating me because her father was a preacher. Perhaps she beat me because I said there were many other solar systems, not just this one. However, I really think she beat me because

15

she was ashamed of her own hair, which was the same colour as mine.

Larry Trueblood. An older boy who lived next door. He was an *albino*. I had to look up what that meant. He would just stand and stare at me or at our house. He never spoke. His right hand was in his right pocket, always. He reminded me of the banjo-playing boy in 'Deliverance' a film which I saw many years later. I never told any of the boys in the house. They would have 'sorted' him. However, when boys 'sort' things, they usually make them worse. You could add Trueblood to my nightmares of dead starlings, Ginger Morgan and snapping turtles.

And now, the worst time.

It was summer. The tree was in full blossom. I was sitting underneath it. It was buzzing with bumblebees. Swallowtail butterflies played above my head. I wasn't visible to anybody. I hear shouting from the small back porch. My mother, always visible because her hair was like a huge red bird. She was crying but not shouting back. Her uncle was standing on the porch shaking his fist at my mother. I never made out his words. I kept invisible in the blossoms, peering through like a hunter in the jungle.

Then I had my best idea, one I thought would save us all. I would escape north, far from starlings, snapping turtles and Ginger Morgan. My mind was clear. Then, my family would come looking for me and follow me, back to where there are ghost bears and no trees, where the grass is green as it should be. We would all be healed.

It was easy. I picked a day when everybody else was busy or away. Answer me this: why are girls often invisible? Nobody even noticed I was gone.

One of my brothers had given me his old scout pack. Perfect. I had a canteen of water. A flashlight. Some chocolate bars and cookies. Matches, one warm waterproof jacket.

Our front door faced north. Pavement. A row of maple trees. A street made of red brick. The dance studio across the street. A path to its right into the Town Park. Tennis and basketball courts, then the huge sledging hill. My brothers and I had already climbed it many times. I was climbing it now. Looking back down the hill, the houses were barely visible above the tall trees: only church spires and steeples were taller than the trees. 'North' was easy during the day and I covered many more miles beyond the summit of the hill, through forests of hedge apples, maple and shagbark hickory.

Come night, I was no longer able to know north from any other direction. I put on the warm jacket and curled up beneath an Osage tree and fell asleep, and dreamed.

Not of Ginger Morgan or snapping turtles. I dreamt of a straight true road, leading through forests until we came to a great river, and then through a forest to a lake which looked like a sea. If I heard wolves howling at night, I knew I was nearly home.

But I had been dreaming. The voices I heard and the flashlight I saw were real. I am a fast runner so I ran and ran. Maybe it was Larry Trueblood or shotgun Clancy?

The park attendant had seen me climbing the hill earlier and when the word went out that I was missing, a search was mounted. It was just him and a policeman. When they took me home, everyone was relieved and angry but mostly relieved. I told them all why I had done it, gone north. Everyone went silent then.

We left the house soon after. Mum, my two brothers and I moved to a smaller house of our own, further north, closer to the hills. The two boys slept in the bedroom while mum and I slept in a sofa bed in the small living room. There was no back door. The front door opened east, where a steady wind sounded like an angry bear trying to force the door open. One early morning I awoke to the wind howling at the door.

I had been dreaming: that I was sitting under the Dogwood. It was full of bees and butterflies. Birds were coming for the berries. Mum was there too, laughing and vibrant. Her hair had grown back, red and luxurious. We were invisible and safe from the outside world; no room for Clancy's starlings or angry hissing reptiles.

Meanwhile, mum slept. The rising sun blazed through our thin curtains, bathing us in its healing light.

MELTING

Alan Bryant

Eight of our shift are left alive; me, four other men and three women. Most of them had families and they have been the worst affected. We all worked together here at the food plant. It was only luck we were in the freezer bay when the sky exploded. Some sort of siren sounded; we wondered if there was a fire next door. There has been a lot of weeping from the women, and from some men too.

I have not cried. There is no-one for me to miss in the old world. There was no-one I wanted to be with that much. I'm better on my own.

For a few, the explosion took out eardrums like fingers through wet tissue. Some have faces coated with dust that has hardened into masks. Their eyes and ears need to be soaked until the shell softens enough to come clear. I was lucky to be wearing industrial goggles and ear defenders and, despite some facial scarring, I have kept my sight and hearing.

We never believed this would happen. Politicians argued, postured, stood and stared to see who would blink first. It was a pageant of egos and desk thumping. Then someone pressed the button and the world got roasted.

Now we are trapped in this creaking wreck of twisted metal. And although the half light seems to muffle our fears and help stop any contagion, inside our heads we must all be screaming.

The outer roof of the building has collapsed and crushed the inner section down from forty feet to a ceiling of about five or six feet in places. Somehow the emergency generator kicked in so we have a few lights but they won't last long. We have no idea of the survival rate outside.

The department foreman, Cecil, has organised things here. We have a communal space about sixty feet square that we cleared of rubble, and there are separate toilet areas. The others collect and huddle together as a group. I suppose this helps to keep their spirits hovering a few inches above floor level.

It took a week to clear our way out but by the time we did that the winds came blasting back. Mini tornados of ash clouds filled with stone and metal fragments cut through the air. The detritus of war flew at us as though fuelled by hate itself. Visibility was almost nil. It was like the world was in a volcanic storm, so now we remain inside. The days are dark grey; there is little light inside or out.

At night I listen to the ice melt, the constant drip, drip, drip of each tiny bead of life hitting the floor. As they cut through the silence I picture the sounds. I see each drip as a crystal in the sunlight of the old world, shining, brilliant. My eyes stay closed as I hold this dream of past, clean sanity.

Then someone begins to sob, mourning the loss of the family they will probably never see again. I stay away from their emotion. I am alive on the outskirts of their sadness. I don't need them.

We have a ready-made food store here in the freezer, but it's all vegetables, most of it is peas. I have survived a nuclear war, now I'm going to die of pea poisoning.

What I need is a burger.

And a shave.

Even more vital than our food, is the water. The freezer ice is melting so we drink as much as we want. The rest we save in containers we salvage.

Maybe I should have got a job in a burger bar.

Instead I sit in this flattened shell in the dimmest light, leaning against a girder that looks like it was bent by manic giants. Between my legs is a bag of peas that are thawing out and almost soft enough to eat without busting a tooth.

When I look around there is a crowd of shoes shuffling about me. I recognise Cecil's size twelve boots. As a supervisor Cecil was OK, a fair man, and I respected him.

"Hi," I say. "I'm sorry, I wasn't expecting company. I'd have heated up the peas."

"We've been talking, Sonny," says Cecil. He talks too loud. He thinks I'm as deaf as he is.

I give what I consider to be a wise nod. "Talking is good," I say. "More talking by our politicians and by now we could have been down town chasing skirt."

The ladies allow me polite, disparaging smiles.

I wave an apologetic arm.

"This stuff is melting," he says.

"Yeah, so at least we can eat it."

"But for how long, Sonny? Soon it'll go mouldy."

I admit I hadn't thought of that. I'm not one for thinking ahead. When I was a kid I wanted to be a fighter pilot but when I realised it wasn't going to work out I decided that planning for the future was over-rated, which is why I ended up wheeling frozen food around.

"So we were thinking," he says. "It's been a week, soon we are going to need to find new food." He pauses, then says, "We need someone to go and find it."

The surrounding feet begin to shuffle anxiously. Out of the shadows Cecil's left foot edges in my direction. I'm finding his feet somehow belligerent today.

I give another series of sage-like nods. However, my respect for authority disappears with surprising speed. "Well screw you, Cecil," I say, "get someone else to find it."

The feet are now shuffling with what I feel could be the beginning of rebellious agitation.

Edgar's voice echoes out. "You've been a trained soldier, Sonny. You're our best chance."

Edgar was a real dickhead when we worked together, making mistakes and blaming me. He wears a ragged, wet bandage over both eyes to help clean the dust out and one of his ear drums has blown. They say his sight is returning but it will be a slow recovery. He grips the arm of Sheila who was a stock-controller here. Like me, Sheila has stayed relatively unharmed. She's not big; she's what you could call well built. You know when you see a quality car, it's put together, sleek, silky, and when you close the car door you hear that reassuring click that means it's solid. Well, Sheila's click is pretty solid too. She's smooth, firm, she has green eyes, and even in this gloom I can see they are looking at me. Her mouth curves gently in a plaintive smile. I realise I'm looking at her and check myself. The other two females also look on with sad, imploring eyes.

The last time I was the centre of attention I was eight years old. My best friend was Polly and one day she put her arms around me. I could feel the tears running down her face. Then she set fire to the mattress and ran off. I was left to take the blame for burning down the care home. Today everyone wants to be my friend. I don't like getting too close to people, they let you down.

Edgar is impatient. He's a small round-shouldered man with short brown hair and a nervous right elbow. "So what do you say, soldier?" he says.

"Actually I was in the Reserves," I say.

Edgar's elbow is twitching. "Are you saying you won't go?"

"Why should I go?"

"We could beat the crap out of you till you agreed." Edgar's elbow is flicking about like it's trying to escape.

"That's really stupid, Edgar." Cecil's voice echoes through the destruction. "Why would he come back with food after that?"

Phoebe speaks. "Please, Sonny, we all have to help each other now." She exaggerates the words in her mouth now her hearing is gone. Phoebe's face is scarred right along one side. She is in her forties and overweight, but I'm guessing our new diet will soon help reduce her dress size. She is knitting a scarf and grips the needles like they are spears to fight off mortality. The scarf has been knitted three times. Each time, before she finishes, she unravels it and starts again. All her hope for continuation of life is in that wool.

"If we can do anything for you Sonny," says Maddie, "you only have to ask."

Maddie is squinting at me because her spectacles were lost in the blast. She is three times my age, and to be honest, unless she's hiding a double cheese burger somewhere, I can't think of much that she could do for me right now.

"That's right, Sonny," says Cecil, "we're all in this together."

A hurried murmur of agreement hums through the dusty air.

Cecil's voice speeds with enthusiasm. "Near here was a canned goods warehouse. There must be enough food in there to last us forever."

"Forever?" I say. "Forever went when they pressed the button, Cecil. Next you'll tell me we're going to rebuild the world. Yeah, I can imagine how the new Bible will start. 'So, faithful readers, when the atomic shit storm ended, the serpent offered up a bag of peas to Cecil. Eat one of these peas', said the serpent, 'and you can screw up this new world the same as you screwed up the old one.' Yeah, Cecil, some Garden of Eden this is."

Sheila starts to cry. The other two women close round her with comforting hugs and whispers. Maybe I've blown my chance with Sheila. I go back to my lunch.

Stavros looks up from his mobile phone. It went flat days ago but he's not giving up on it. He has one eye bandaged. Stavros was the union man here till the world went nuclear. "We must keep a united front, Sonny," he says. "We can't show those bastards any weakness. Our brothers the world over -."

I hold up my hand to stop him talking right there. I'm not sure who he means by 'those bastards' but I don't question him. If I'm going to die here I'd rather starve than do it listening to a marathon on Karl Marx's philosophies.

"God will bring you back to us." Joseph says. Joseph is a lay-preacher and well-meaning haemophiliac. The fact that Joseph is not only still alive but came through it all without a scratch must prove that miracles can happen. He puts his hands together. "We will pray for you, Sonny."

24

More hurried assent murmurs around me.

"We found this, Sonny," says Cecil. "The hygiene people must have left it last time they cleaned the place."

I look up. Cecil holds a white nylon zip-suit with built-in shoes, gloves and visor.

"This can protect you from the dust."

He holds it out to me. His demeanour shows an awkwardness I've never noticed before. "It's midday," he says, "you should have enough light to find your way around outside."

There is a hesitant silence.

"I always had you down as a good man, Sonny," Cecil says.

Thinking about it, I've got no choice. I'm going to need a new source of food anyway. I might be asking myself why I did this for the rest of my life, however long that will be, but I get up and take the suit from him. Sheila stops crying.

I breathe deep, put the suit on, and wonder what I'm going to find out there. Amid some good luck calls of forced enthusiasm I walk to the doorway to Hell.

It's a steel emergency door that opens out onto the world, or whatever is left of the world. We had to unbolt the hinges the first time because it was jammed but after straightening out a few angles we wedged it back. Now we prise it open again.

"Knock when you're ready to come back in," says Cecil.

"Thanks for the invitation," I say, and step outside. The door clangs shut with panic ringing through its echo.

"Bring it back, soldier," shouts Edgar.

I look back with a fleeting wish that his balls explode then adjust my eyes to the light. Visibility has improved to about twenty yards, but my visor mists up straight away so I ease it open. The world has an orange tinge and the air drifts with ash and smells burnt. Some buildings are still smouldering but it feels cold. The wind behind me gives a low, eerie whistling and though it has slowed it's still gusting.

Maybe I'm better off on my own out here. That's how I've always managed best.

Grey-brown powder covers everything. It's like someone emptied the clouds but it's ash, flowing like a smooth duvet desert. It's enticing, as if saying, 'Lie down on me, I'll keep you warm.' I imagine myself wallowing into it with Sheila. We're naked, covered in ash and peas. Jeez. No, I've got to concentrate.

Every building is damaged or flat. Those still standing lean away, bowing like desecrated sculptures of surrender. I look over to where the canned food warehouse should be but it's not visible so I start to walk. I'm kicking up clouds of dust, leaving a trail a blind man could follow. Our main industrial town was ten miles away to the east, so I'm guessing the blast has done even more damage there. The world is a wilderness; a dry, powdered junkyard. Burnt-out vehicles are strewn about in heaps. Charred body parts poke through the dust; scattered limbs, grotesque heads. I expect them to rise up at any time so I stay wary. I've seen films like this where people kill for a busted teabag.

A shape appears through the haze. It's a low lump of what could have been a building. I head to it and walk around the wreckage. Finding a gap I look inside. Like the freezer plant, the interior was sheltered and the roof is crushed. Inside it's dark, but I see bodies. This is my first sight of dead people still in one piece. Seven or eight of them look like they have been blasted through the air. They hang limp across mangled

26

frameworks. Now there is a stronger smell in my nostrils. It's the stench of decay and wasted lives. I want to run, I want to vomit, but the first action would be pointless and the second inadvisable in a one piece suit.

And I need food, so I go inside.

In the darkness I think I see something move. There is no sound, no shadow. A second later I'm pushed from behind. I land face down thudding into the ash. I try to look up but the dust is too thick. Something, somebody is raining blows down onto my back with what feels like a sledge hammer.

Using all my strength I twist onto my side and curl up foetal style for protection. I look up and see a shadow. Arms are flailing above me. Now it's screaming. It's a mess of blows, dust and noise. My insides are knotted. I'm breathing adrenaline, looking for directions of escape. I've been hurt before so I'm scared. But I'm guessing my attacker is scared too. I manage to roll away and crawl behind a pile of busted panelling. The figure follows me, still pounding away.

I'm going to die here. A thousand years from now my body will be dug up and dissected by archaeologists. One will turn to another and say, 'Look at this, his insides have been mashed up. And check this out, this guy has got peas in his DNA.'

The noise goes on but I'm not getting hurt anymore. I look over and see him. He's holding something, smashing it into the ground. He stops. He's realised I've escaped. He's stretching his arms out trying to touch something. I watch him. He's been blinded.

I've always had a fear of losing my sight. Being blind must be like not being able to see the future when the future is already there looking at you, like a secret place everyone knows about except you.

"I know where you are," he says. The words grate, parched, from his throat.

As I start to get up he rushes at me. He must be some sort of man-bat who can see by sound waves. No, he runs straight into a horizontal girder that drops him like a sack of proverbial. He's down, he's bleeding from the head but I think he's alive. In his hand is a food can. That must be what he hit me with so I grab it before he recovers. As I do, another crazy man's voice is screaming at me. "Get off my friend." I'm hurled forward again. My visor breaks off and my face is being pushed into the dust. I duck and twist around to use his momentum against him and he gets flung on to the remains of a wall. I'm getting my breath back as he lays on the floor groaning.

I drop the can and shout, "OK, listen. I'm not here to hurt anybody." I go back to the first man who is trying to lift himself off the floor. He turns his face to me; it's crusted with ash. He's old, wearing ragged clothes. His hair was white, now it's grey-brown with dust. His hands wander through the air trying to find something to cling to.

"Are you one of them Martians?" he says.

"What? No, do I look like a Martian?"

He looks up with his blind eyes. "Well, how the fuck would I know?"

Looking at my suit I concede that point in silence.

His hands go up to his bleeding head. "Craggo reckons the Martians blew us up."

"Craggo?"

"You just met him."

28

"That maniac?"

"He's my buddy. We worked here. Did the Martians do this?"

"No our politicians did this."

"They did?" He shakes his head. "Bastards. They're supposed to be on our side."

"Yeah, that'll teach you not to trust people who tell you to trust them."

"So why should I trust you?" He sits up holding his head.

"Believe me, I'm Sonny. I'm from the freezer plant next door. We have water."

"You have water?"

"Yeah. So who are you?"

"Griff."

"OK, Griff. Show me the cans, then I'll take you back with me."

"You're lying."

He lunges for me but I sidestep him. I'm losing patience now. I take a guess but I suppose if Edgar's sight is coming back then we could do the same for him. "Listen," I say, "We can make you see again."

"You can't do that."

"Yes, we can. Believe me."

"You keep saying that."

"We can do it. First, I need to find the food, then we'll get back to the freezer. Soon you'll have water and we'll get to work on your eyes."

By now Craggo is groaning and starting to get up off the floor. I move away to catch my breath and wait until he is standing. As I watch him try to stand he keeps on getting higher. Upright he's a seven feet tall yeti of a man. If he kicks off again I'm out of here and they can keep their food cans.

Looking at his face I see one side of it is burned. "Look at me, Craggo. I know you can see me." When he turns to me I look in his eyes. It's like looking for the moon on a cloudy night, you know it's there somewhere but the light won't show. He's shivering with fear. I think it could be my suit. I look like a cheap Buzz Aldrin impersonator, or, yes, possibly a Martian. I hold out my hands, palms facing him. "I'm not a Martian, Craggo. I worked in the freezer plant. My name is Sonny. Can you see me?"

His face is blank. With some caution I reach out to give him a tentative shake. "Craggo, show me where the food is, then we can all get out of here and go for a nice cool drink of water. Would you like that? Water?"

He licks his cracked lips then tries to spit, but he can't. He nods again.

"Help me with Griff," I say. "You know Griff, don't you? He's a friend, right?"

Slowly he nods. "My friend," he mumbles.

"That's right, and I'm your friend too, so we're all friends, right?" I think he nods but no matter, I've got to get out of here soon. "OK, Craggo, show me the cans and let's all get from here. So where are they?"

He points to the interior.

We help Griff to his feet and manoeuvre ourselves across jagged steelwork to get further inside the wreckage. I keep an eye on the daylight at the entrance behind us. Once that light disappears I will be totally dependent on my new companions. That's not an ideal situation for a suspected Martian in the company of two maniacs.

We struggle deeper into the wreckage. When the daylight behind me disappears I stop. Griff falls to his knees. Craggo is staggering in front of me, still pointing the way.

"OK," I say, "where exactly is the food?"

The whole place is a mess. Craggo points to a heap of charred and busted crates. The cans have exploded. It looks like someone has emptied a cement mixer and left it to solidify. When I touch it, it's rock hard.

"Where are the other cans? This was a canned food warehouse."

"They're gone," says Griff. "Destroyed."

"Gone? There must be something left?" I search the darkness for signs of cans. All I see is hardened rivers of food covered in ash. "None left at all?"

"Only that one I hit you with," Griff says, "but you threw it away."

"One can?" Now I'm shouting. "I came here for one lousy can?"

My shouting has frightened Craggo. He starts to scream. He is uncontrollable, spinning in wild circles till he topples over onto the floor. Seconds later he's grabbing hold of anything within reach to stand up. As he stands erect he stretches and goes ballistic again. All I can do is watch as he tries to chew through a girder.

I try to sound like this is an every-day situation. "Griff," I say, "is Craggo OK?" It's obvious he isn't but psychological diagnosis was never my strong point.

"No," he says, "his nerves are shot."

"Yeah? Well any minute now mine will be too." I take a deep breath.

"Give him a hug." Griff says, "He does this sometimes, but he'll be OK."

"A hug?"

"You're too shy?"

"Why would I give him a hug?"

Griff's voice rises. "It'll calm him down. Hug him."

"You're kidding. You're as crazy as he is."

Griff's voice is barking with urgency. "Hug him. It's the only thing that stops him."

I walk around until I'm standing behind Craggo. All I can do is stare at this huge, mad creature and wonder what he will do next. My voice finally finds its way out of my throat. "Griff, I'm not sure about this."

"Do it!"

My instinct tells me to back off. I'm wondering how long I can keep delaying this. "Tell you what, Griff."

"What?"

"Couldn't I just high five him?"

Griff's voice is splintering. "Do it before he hurts himself!"

I force my legs to move. I'm three feet away with arms open wide. I freeze again. Craggo turns and rushes me with a roar that must vie for the throat clearance of the season. He's up against me, pounding the air with his fists. I'm no match for his strength.

Griff is on the floor screaming. "Put your arms around him. Hug him."

I shut my eyes and clamp my arms around his body. I'm bouncing around holding onto him. If I let go he will fling me away like a rag.

Griff is screaming. "Hug him. Tighter."

My arms grip him. I pull him in closer, tighter. As I do it's like a warm, melting softness passes between us. Craggo slows his wild convulsing actions. They become gentle swaying movements. A strange calming seems to float through my chest. I pass this off as some sort of adrenaline fade. When he stops he moans, his head rests on mine. We stay like that for some minutes till his breathing slows.

"You can let him go now," says Griff, "he'll be fine."

I know at some point I must break away from my new buddy. After all this I don't want Craggo thinking I have intentions of buying a ring. But I have to decide when it's safe to do this. In a series of slow movements I relax my grip and lower my arms. I take a long pace back, then another one. Craggo's head is down. He is silent, unmoving. I come out for food and end up with a pair of crazies. In the most measured voice I can manage I say, "OK, let's find that one and only can and get from here."

Now I'm not alone but have two lunatics to manhandle. What am I doing here? Why am I even thinking of taking anyone back with me? Jeez. If a man can't go for a quiet walk after Armageddon when can he?

Outside the wind is blowing straight at us now and I'm without a visor. But following my trail through the dust is not difficult, and we head back to the freezer building. Craggo doesn't seem to notice the cooked limbs or the skulls in the dust. I don't think he sees much at all. Griff carries our only can. He falls every few yards and I get weaker each time I lift him. My body feels like it's been through a crusher and with every step I wonder why I'm taking these men with me. Maybe I'm as crazy as they are. My popularity rating is going to take a real hit when I get them back to the others.

At the freezer entrance I shout for them to open the door. I'm holding Griff around his waist with my left arm. Craggo grips my right arm. I kick the door and shout again. There is an eye peeping out at us through a gap in the wall, then some shuffling inside but nothing else happens. I lose patience and kick the door again.

Griff turns out to be a man of even less patience. He finds the strength to throw himself at the building. But his tattered, old body bounces off the metal and he crumples in a heap.

I hoist him back on his feet. He is leaning against me, panting. Craggo's grip is turning into a tourniquet. I'm watching my fingers change colour.

Cecil shouts from inside. "You want us to let that crazy man in here?"

"I've got two weak men here. All they want is water. Open the door."

Edgar calls next. "What if they try to hurt us?"

"No chance." I say. "There are more of us than them. Open the door before we kick it in."

There is another faint deliberation from inside. We wait. A minute later they start to prise open the door. I ease Griff in first with the can. Then Craggo and I go in like we're conjoined. When we're all inside they pull the door shut and it's bolted tight. My eyes adjust to the darkness as the group assembles around us. Craggo has moved back to stand behind me now, his arms vice locked around my chest. It would take another nuclear attack to loosen his grip.

"These men need water," I say. "Griff needs his eyes bathed. He can't see."

"So where is the food, Sonny?" Cecil checks the three of us over as if looking for can sized bulges in our pockets.

34

I nod to Griff. "There it is."

"One can?" says Cecil, taking it from Griff.

"You bring one can and two extra mouths to feed?" says Edgar. "We should throw them back out there." His elbow is starting to jerk about. Now he runs straight at me.

Craggo's grip gets even tighter on me. His voice is shivering. "Don't hurt him," he says, "I'll kill you."

This is the first time in my life anyone offered to protect me. I thought I was looking after Craggo; it turns out he's my minder. I feel like I'm an honoured guest here.

Edgar retreats back to Sheila. She gives me a smile that combines relief with disbelief.

"Sonny was right to bring them," says Cecil, "we all have to look out for each other now."

Phoebe grips her part-knitted scarf. Joseph blesses the can of food and Stavros checks his watch before writing something on his phone keypad. Normality has a new meaning.

Griff's arms stretch out seeking some invisible guide to lead him away to the light.

Maddie takes hold of him. "Come on, we'll get you to see again."

"You will?" says Griff. "You can make me see again?"

Maddie pats his arm. "It might take a while but we can do it."

His voice croaks up a notch. "That's amazing, I haven't been able to see for thirty years. Thank you, thank you everyone."

A silence descends as we look at him, and each other. Maybe my promise of regained sight was too hasty.

Then I see Griff allow himself the beginnings of a smile. He is still locked in his own despair, but this one subtle gesture conveys an air of impish mischief, and possibly the slightest notion of contentment at his being amongst people again.

Maddie coaxes him forward. "We'll do what we can."

Griff knows he is not going to see. Maybe he thinks there are more important things in life now.

He stops and half turns. His voice is a cracked whisper. "Sonny, is Craggo with you?"

Craggo is still squeezing the life from me. If my skeleton had a white flag it would be waving it now. I'm gasping. "He's with me, Griff."

"Look after him for me will you?"

"I will, Griff."

"You promise?"

"Yes, I promise."

"Thank you, Sonny." He turns to Maddie. "Craggo's had a tough time, he's not thinking too straight."

Maddie looks at me, and though we have two more survivors today her eyes still glisten with the soft sadness of loss.

Sheila leaves me with a pale smile and in her eyes I see a quick reflection of what could be the glinting light of encouragement. The group meanders back into the crushed maze. As Maddie leads Griff away he talks to her, "Hey," he says, "these two men, they're my friends. Isn't that right, Sonny?"

"That's right, Griff, we're friends." As I say this, Craggo's grip begins to relax. In an automatic gesture of relief my lungs manage a half choked chorus of gratitude. I give a reassuring squeeze to his arm, and he nods in acknowledgement of our friendship.

36

Now it is quiet, all I hear is the water dripping away. I begin to wonder how long our water will last, how many others are out there without water.

"By the way, Griff," I say, "any idea of what is in that can?"

His voice croaks back to me. "We only ever stored peas."

TEA AND BISCUITS

Paul B. Cohen

Evelyn Parkinson made it a habit to attend Sunday morning concerts at the Wigmore Hall. The programme was a pleasing length, with no overpowering symphonic music to threaten the serenity of the weekend. After the performance, one could choose between a free orange juice and a glass of sherry. Occasionally, Evelyn spoke to another concertgoer, and then departed into the hurly-burly of London.

One October morning, she found an intriguing reference in the programme. The pianist, Richard Watson, would be performing Chopin and Poulenc. Glancing at his biography, she read that the Polish teacher Lazar Weinberg had taught Watson. She noted that fact particularly, because, for a short time when she was a child, Mr Weinberg had been very familiar to her. As an adult, however, she had scarcely thought of the man.

Now, seeing Weinberg's name in print, she thought of him. She remembered the baldpate he had; she remembered his absurd paisley slippers. And she remembered the sorrow that lurked in his eyes, usually masked by a jocular demeanour.

Post-concert, Evelyn wondered if Richard Watson was still in the building. Lingering for a few minutes with her drink, she observed the stage door opening, and Watson, in shirt and jeans, appeared. Evelyn did not want to intrude, yet she could not curb the impulse to approach.

"Mr Watson? Can I say that I enjoyed your playing very much," Evelyn said.

"Thank you," the musician replied.

"And I read Lazar Weinberg was once your teacher."

"He was indeed. Did he teach you?"

"Oh no – I never learned piano. He was our neighbour in Highgate when I was a child."

Watson raised his eyebrow. "That's where he taught me."

"Then you might have even practiced when we lived in the flat above," Evelyn said.

"How funny! But I didn't have him as a teacher long enough," Watson replied. "I only wish I could have trebled my time with him."

For Evelyn, the bus ride home to Islington was soaked with recollections. She remembered being an eight-year-old in Highgate. One afternoon, when the winter's gloom threatened to depress spirits, her mother summoned her to the kitchen. Thinking back, Evelyn could picture the crimson of her mother's knitted cardigan, the precarious state of the water jug on the shelf above the sink, and the calendar pinned onto the refrigerator with its bucolic scenes of the British countryside.

"Evie," her mother said, "I've an errand for you. I want you to take this to Mr Weinberg." Her mother indicated their Windsor Castle tray. "There's a pot of tea and a plate of my ginger biscuits for him."

The girl was puzzled. "Now?"

"Yes, now. Go carefully down the stairs with the tray."

Evelyn did not see why her mother couldn't take her biscuits herself, but as she'd always been curious about their neighbour, she was content to fulfil the errand. What was more, she was keen to see inside Mr Weinberg's flat. She liked to see other people's homes whenever she could. She thought she might become an architect when she grew up.

She picked up the tray and remembered how she had been taught to walk 'like a lady'. This meant one precise step after another, whilst keeping her eyesight level. She hoped she was becoming adept at such manoeuvres.

One floor below, Evelyn approached Mr Weinberg's door, listening for melodies. Setting the tray on the tufted 'welcome' mat, she knocked. No reply. She tried again, noticing the stillness of the milky brown tea at her feet. Her mother's biscuits – three of them – were displayed on a Royal Doulton plate, one with blue swirls around the rim. She knocked afresh.

"Is open. Come," a voice called.

Evelyn turned the handle and entered. The hallway in front of her was carpeted in burgundy, its walls a parade of framed photographs. She knew where to go, since the flat's layout mirrored her own home, and veered right into the lounge. The room's furniture contrasted with her family's austere furnishings. There was a green carpet underfoot, wrought iron lighting that seemed to drip from the ceiling, gold drapes that made her think of a desert tent from 'The Arabian Nights', and an imposing piano.

In an armchair sat Lazar Weinberg. He had a dark suit on, an unbuttoned waistcoat, and a cravat. Despite his formal attire, he wore slippers that made his feet look huge. His hands were folded in his lap.

"I've brought you tea and biscuits," Evelyn said. "From my mother."

"I can see," said Mr Weinberg. "She told me she would be sending you with this."

"Mum made the biscuits herself, Mr Weinberg."

He chuckled. "Ah. Homemade is always best, yes?"

"Well, she can't stand buying them from shops."

"Put them here," the piano teacher said, pointing to a side table.

"They're ginger, the biscuits," she explained.

Lazar Weinberg got out of his chair, chose a biscuit, and crunched. "Very ginger. Here, take a bite."

She shook her head. "They're for you."

"Don't you like them?" he teased.

"Oh, I love them," she said, "but I can't have one now. It's too near my dinnertime."

"You are well behaved, my dear."

The praise embarrassed her. "I'll come back for the tray later," Evelyn said.

"Fine. Please see yourself out, if you don't mind. I have a boy coming in a minute or two. Very promising student, this one."

Upstairs, Evelyn sought her mother out to report back. "I took everything to Mr Weinberg."

"Good," Mrs Parkinson said, peering into her oven.

"Doesn't he know how to make tea himself?"

"It's not that. I don't know if he eats."

"He must do," Evelyn insisted. "Everyone eats, don't they?"

"He teaches one pupil after another, all day. Perhaps I'll make scones for him."

"And for us?" the girl asked. She loved her mother's scones even more than the ginger biscuits.

An hour later, Evelyn returned for the Windsor Castle tray. Lazar Weinberg was in a chair at the piano, teaching a stub-nosed girl in a lengthy orange dress.

Evelyn noticed that one biscuit had not been eaten. The piano teacher read her look. "The biscuits were delicious. Two were enough. Give your mother my great thanks."

Going up the stairs, Evelyn stared at the blue plate. One biscuit. She wanted it, and worked out that perhaps she could have it. Her mother would think that Mr Weinberg had eaten all three. It wouldn't really spoil her appetite at dinner, and who would know?

She whipped out a hand and crammed the biscuit in her mouth. She munched silently, as if the clash of her teeth might broadcast her theft to the world.

When she had cleared her mouth of evidence, Evelyn walked back into her flat, setting the tray, drained cup, and crumb-dotted plate, on the kitchen counter.

The following afternoon, Evelyn repeated her pilfering, but this time she pounced before taking the tray to Mr Weinberg. Once she was sure her mother had shut the door, she halted on the stairs, and ate one of the three biscuits on the plate. They were delightful.

Every day that week, Evelyn delivered two biscuits and a cup of tea, enjoying her clandestine treat of the third biscuit on the stairs between home and Mr Weinberg's flat. And every day, she relished the fact that her mother did not know what she was doing.

One afternoon, Mr Weinberg said, "I was wondering how old you are."

"I'm nine," Evelyn said. "I turn ten in July."

"Is that so? My birthday is also in July."

"Perhaps we can have a joint birthday party," she suggested.

"You are a lovely child, Evelyn," he said, creasing his mouth into a smile.

At ease in the apartment, Evelyn felt comfortable enough to ask a question of her own. "Where do you come from, Mr Weinberg?" she asked.

"I'm from Poland."

"Where's that?"

"Eastern Europe. Quite a long way from here."

Evelyn shuffled her feet. "Do you have a wife?"

Lazar hesitated. The girl noticed that he was gripping one hand with the other, and that his fingernails blanched under the pressure.

"I did, yes."

Evelyn sensed she should not ask any more. "I think I'll go back upstairs."

Mr Weinberg followed her to the door. "You know," he said, his breath warm on her, "I also did once have a girl who was nine."

She could sense the sadness in his voice. "You don't now, do you?"

"No, Evelyn, I don't."

Evelyn fidgeted. "Did she look like me?"

Mr Weinberg pointed to a small black and white photograph of a child. "That's her. Take a look ... I think you can see she wasn't like you. For instance, you have fair hair, and hers was very dark. But she smiled in a charming way, as you do."

"How many teeth had she lost by the time she was nine?"

"I don't know, Evelyn," Lazar said, his voice tinged with melancholy. "I don't recall. How many have you lost?"

"I've lost count," said Evelyn.

"Don't lose count of the things no longer with you. Remember that."

The girl didn't understand what the music teacher meant, but she nodded out of politeness.

The incident that became engraved in Evelyn's memory took place on a day of blazing weather. Despite the heat, Mr Weinberg continued to wear his jacket, cravat, and slippers. Evelyn, meanwhile, sported sleeveless dresses, and on that day, her frock was light pink, with polka dots all over.

In his apartment, the golden drapes resisted the sunlight, and the electric lights burned, as they always did. No pupil was at the keyboard. Mr Weinberg was reclining in his armchair, hands interlinked on his lap. There was a petrifying moment when Evelyn thought the old man might have passed away, but she saw that his breathing was as rhythmical as a slow waltz. She was relieved when she understood he was only sleeping.

She put the tray down. The three ginger biscuits presented themselves to her. Evelyn looked around. She saw the immobile metronome on top of the piano. She glanced at the oil painting of Paris on the wall, its citizens scurrying in the drizzly rain. Her eyes scoured the sheet music on the piano, before returning to the tray, and specifically the Royal Doulton plate. She knew she could not resist. She reached and took a first biscuit, chomping it deftly. She snatched a second biscuit, and ran it along her teeth. It came away in delectable bits at the front of her mouth. Finally, she picked up the third biscuit and put it onto her tongue, letting it dissolve, all the while checking Mr Weinberg, to be certain he was still asleep.

Her mouth awash with ginger and sugar, Evelyn returned to her home to find Aunt Caroline and her mother sitting in the lounge. She was allowed to sit with them and play whilst the women chatted. Several hours passed, and Evelyn forgot to go down to Lazar Weinberg's flat for the tray.

Around six o'clock, Evelyn was idling through a sequel to 'Heidi', waiting for dinner, when there was a knock on the door.

"Hello, Mr Weinberg," her mother said.

"Good afternoon, Mrs Parkinson."

"How nice to see you. Won't you come in?"

"I have a pupil in a moment, so I won't stay," he replied. "I have your tea things here."

"Oh, Evie forgot to fetch them. I'm so sorry," Mrs Parkinson said.

"No need to be sorry. This gives me the chance to thank you for being so generous, every day, when you send the little one with your special delivery."

Mrs Parkinson took the tray from the music teacher. "It's a pleasure for both of us, Mr Weinberg, to bring you a very English treat."

Evelyn had put down her book. Something about how the conversation was unfolding was not to her liking.

"I love seeing that plate empty, Mr Weinberg," Evelyn's mother said.

"Your biscuits are so enjoyable that I missed them today," the piano teacher replied.

"Missed them?" Evelyn's mother asked. "I put them on the Royal Doulton plate, as usual."

"I think I was taking a nap when Evelyn arrived. When I opened my eyes, the drink was warm, but your plate had nothing on it."

"How curious, Mr Weinberg," she said. "I'm sorry about that. I'll make sure you have them tomorrow."

"I look forward to it. If you don't mind, I must go back down now."

"Evelyn?" Mrs Parkinson called, after closing the front door. "Could you come here?"

It was a momentary business for the truth to be revealed, and Evelyn was sent to her room to await her father's return from work. She had been scolded, but not smacked. She wet her pillow with tears. Why had Mr Weinberg brought up the tray and told her mother about the missing biscuits? Did he want to land her in trouble? Was he horrible, underneath that kindly manner?

She found no answer to these questions. She would not admit to herself that leaving the tray downstairs had led to the discovery of her actions; she preferred to blame the piano teacher.

For the next two days, Mrs Parkinson delivered Mr Weinberg's tea and biscuits. Evelyn longed to resume her duties, but dared not ask her mother for permission. The following Monday, however, Evelyn sensed that her punishment was over.

In the kitchen, her mother held her arm for a moment. "I know you love my biscuits, Evelyn, but there's never a reason to steal, is there?"

Downstairs, as she carried the tray towards the piano, she wanted to ask Mr Weinberg why he had told her mother about the empty plate. He was engrossed with a student, however, and Evelyn did not disturb him.

She left the flat having uttered not a word to the teacher. The task had felt empty, or merely dutiful, without the reward of her secret treat.

Only a week later, everything changed, because her mother told her that they would be moving to Finchley at the weekend. This was sudden, and Evelyn wondered why her mother had not spoken to her about it, and why she had not even noticed her parents packing their belongings.

When Evelyn was in her first year of university, her mother happened to mention during their weekly phone call that Lazar Weinberg had passed away, and that there was a small obituary in 'The Daily Telegraph'.

Evelyn had not seen him since those childhood days.

On the Sunday evening following Richard Watson's Wigmore Hall recital, Evelyn phoned her aunt. Her mother had been dead for five years, so it helped that she was close to Aunt Caroline. She needed a recipe.

"I've looked through mum's cookbook, but it's not in there," Evelyn said.

"For ginger biscuits? I think we can sort out the recipe between us," Caroline replied.

Under her aunt's dictation, Evelyn wrote down the modest list of ingredients. Next, she went to Richard Watson's website and sent him a message. She wanted to know if he had any idea where Lazar Weinberg was buried. Then she did some research on the piano teacher. He had survived the Auschwitz death camp. His wife, Malka, and daughter Sara, had not.

47

Evelyn received a reply from Watson the next day: "He's at Hoop Lane. It's a cemetery in Golders Green. I went to the funeral. Best regards, Richard Watson."

The following afternoon, she left work earlier than usual, and rode the tube to Golders Green, holding a carrier bag. A woman outside the station told her to take the 82 bus, and she asked the driver for Hoop Lane.

She hesitated at the entrance to the cemetery, finding the stolid red brick entrance foreboding. She had not expected it to be so large a site, and wondered how she would locate the grave she needed.

An office nearby threw out a diffuse light. Inside, a middle-aged man with a black beard was studying an enormous ledger.

Without looking up, he asked, "May I help you?"

"I'm looking for the grave of someone I once knew," said Evelyn.

A few minutes later, with a slip of paper containing a row letter and plot number, Evelyn picked her way between gray and shiny black headstones. She was surprised that some of the stones were laid flat, whereas others – older ones – stood upright, with lettering in what she assumed was Hebrew.

Lazar Weinberg's grave stood at the end of a row. For some reason, there was an unpretentious row of pebbles in front of his headstone; she had expected flowers.

"Hello, Mr Weinberg," she said. "It's Evelyn Parkinson."

Evelyn removed a folding stool from her bag. She poured herself tea from a flask. She was not sure that it was acceptable to drink in the cemetery, but as there was nobody around, she went ahead.

48

"I hope you don't mind me saying, but I always wondered why you told my mother about those missing biscuits. I don't think you wanted to get me in trouble..." She gazed at Weinberg's grave, groping for a conclusion. "I think you just liked the truth, even if I didn't, at the time."

Evelyn took out a cling-wrapped blue Royal Doulton plate, with three biscuits on it. One by one, she placed the biscuits on top of the headstone.

"Here are the biscuits I stole from you that time, Mr Weinberg," she said. "I've made some others, but they're not as good as my mother's. Sorry about that."

The rain was more intent now. "I read about your wife and child, Mr Weinberg," she murmured. "I hope you're with them now."

After finishing her tea, and munching one of her remaining biscuits, she packed up. With the taste of sugar and ginger on her tongue, Evelyn headed for home, putting one precise foot in front of the other.

ROUTE OF FLIGHT

Aoife Inman

The car had broken down just off the main drag. Nathaniel had been behind the wheel, Greta riding shotgun, when the pedals guttered and choked, finally giving in on a clean slice of monotonous road the locals called The Downs. It was like a stretch of American highway transplanted to the fringes of England's south coast. At least, it was just how Greta imagined American highways to look. She'd seen those faux Westerns enough times to recognize the landscape, the red earth, the flat grasslands to the right and left, the moon like an orb above the white centre line. There were, of course, fewer cacti here than in Nevada, she imagined, but the ground was barren enough to become a Western playground for those with enough imagination. The Downs matched up to the movies, almost, if you squinted against the sun. Regardless, it was an exotic wasteland; special in the eyes of those who could imagine it to be so. On either side of the strip of road, low, dry bushes stretched for yards and yards, speckled with heather and gorse, a smattering of yellow flowers that blanketed the empty plains. In the summer months, under a cloudless midday sun, mirages clotted like shallow tide pools across the tarmac.

In many ways it was the perfect place for your brakes to give in. The level miles of tarmac ensured a slow, controlled halt. Still the timing was less than ideal. They had been driving back to the little whitewash holiday cottage they were renting for the summer. It was a slip of a place, nestled in a backwater

50

village, a hair's breadth from the cold sting of the Atlantic and a twenty-minute drive from civilisation or a decent coffee shop. Greta's father knew the couple that let it out; old school friends, he'd told her on the phone.

"Used to fish with him and his dad, good bloke he is … and his wife, Ann? Only best friends with Jo … our Jo, you know?"

She knew of course, but she pretended she didn't. Not for any reason other than to cut the conversation short. It was an excuse to replace the receiver and escape any further discussion of her former home. It was petty really but that sort of familiarity, the kind her father cherished, seemed the curse of these small enclaves, or at least that was how Greta viewed it, as a curse. These villages, the sort that she had spent the best part of her youth in, seemed to trap people, cocooning them until twenty years had passed and the thought of leaving seemed absurd. In these parts, those who'd 'made it' married near strangers from the west coast or spent a handful of years in a northern powerhouse studying marine science or chemical engineering, only to return home, deflated. Still, despite her resentment of small town living, the familial connections to the region had granted them friendly rental rates in prime season. It was difficult to resent that at least.

As the car had juddered to a halt, they had sighed. They were less than half a mile from the cottage. Their destination seemed unpleasantly tangible as they pushed the coughing motor to the road's edge, out of harm's reach. For all its strange ideality, The Downs was a notorious site for pile-ups and fatalities, cars upended in rally races, their passengers deposited meters from their vehicles. It was the nature of the road. The plain of tarmac stretched like a runway, it made your feet itch on the pedals, daring you to be reckless.

The day itself had been hot, baking in fact, 'an Indian summer' they'd called it on the radio that morning, and Greta's legs and arms shone raw with the heat of the sun. Now, in the stationary car, they began to itch, swelling scarlet under the darkening sky. She scrabbled for a tube of aloe in the foot-well of the passenger seat, embalming her skin with it. Slathered in the cool jelly, she shook off her shoes and socks and stepped out onto the road, hopping up onto the bumper to recline against the windshield.

"Think we could walk it from here?" Nat passed her a cigarette, blowing smoke into the air between them as he talked. She declined. She hated his smoking. She hated the smell, the clawing ashy scent that lingered at his perimeters despite copious sticks of gum. The heat made the smell worse. It mingled with their sweat, making it sticky and sweet.

"Probably." She shrugged leaning up onto her shoulder to face him. He stared up at the sky, deep in thought.

"Can't just leave the car though, can we? Not here anyway," she added after a beat.

He ignored her, drawing on his fag. "How long do you reckon it'd take us?"

As he spoke, wisps of smoke trailed from between the gaps in his teeth, dissolving in the red air.

"20, 30 minutes I reckon."

She exhaled loudly, heaving herself upright to sit, out of reach of his ashy breath, legs swinging from the bonnet.

They waited in silence for a while, her sitting, him laid out on the front of the car, limbs loose. An adder slithered past. Her eyes watched as its mossy back zigzagged across the road, looking for the safety of the dry grass. She sympathised with its desperate shuffling plea for escape in a pitiful, self-depreciating sort of way. 'You and me both,' she thought, 'you and me both.' She shifted her feet sideways, clearing it a runway to the heath beyond. The Downs was crawling with animals, adders and grass snakes, hares and a handful of scruffy ex-house cats. Greta had always favoured the snakes though. She felt they added to the exoticism of the place, making the road and the gorse marshes feel dangerous, a desert of sorts; like the outback it was a landscape that could swallow you whole.

In the Australian outback people could go missing for days. A few years ago Greta had developed a morbid fascination with tracking those cases. She had been in-between sources of incomes and thus faced an expanse of unregulated afternoons at her disposal, so she had trailed stories of disappeared backpackers and motorcyclists through news forums and chat-rooms, interviews and obituaries. There were tens of them a year, she discovered, if you really scoured the papers. There were tourists who'd run out of fuel, hikers disorientated by the thumping heat of the sun, or those who simply cut all ties and vanished. She'd found herself trawling the Internet for them, chasing news threads like powder highs. She couldn't really understand it herself at first, why she scored off other people's loss. That's what they were after all, these bodies that turned up on Australian dirt tracks bleached by the sun.

They were husbands and wives, brothers and sons, a fact that got lost mostly though, amid the horrors.

Nathaniel had his opinions of course, said her interest in it was sick, voicing his concern over copious glasses of cheap wine. He blamed her misplaced curiosity on 'emotional trauma', and never her current state of unemployment. She had to be broken, not bored. Greta had tuned out at some point in the discussion, letting him slur on with his diagnosis, nudging the wine bottle just beyond reach. He concluded that she hadn't sufficiently dealt with the reality of her own bereavement, that her fascination with death was part of the grieving process.

She had been eight when they found the cancer. Pancreatic, a secondary tumour, rotten luck they'd said. Prognosis was four months; her mother had lasted three, the cells multiplying soundlessly beneath the round of her stomach, spreading like spores. They ate her mother from the inside out. She shrank visibly before them, fat slipping from her limbs, until one day everyone was crying.

For a few weeks relatives with red eyes fed Greta frozen chips and bags of jelly snakes, delivering her glitter gel-pens and VHS tapes to occupy her so they could weep in peace. Then, eventually, life moved on. The guests faded back into their own lives and Greta and her father simply began again. She felt sad, sure, but there were school trips and birthdays, graduations and screaming rows that dampened the loss. She missed her mother like a stranger, but that was it, no traumatic wound, no unresolved pain. She was just a kid without a mum. Like half her classmates she was one parent down.

But Nat insisted on his theories, informed her that she needed therapy. Greta let him know what she thought, told him that was bull and told him where to stick his undergraduate psychology crap. "Stop analysing me like some rat in a cage," she said.

And that was that. They didn't talk about it again. It was dismissed as another bleary argument, the perimeters of blame not worth defining.

Within a month or so she had a new job, a new distraction, as the legal assistant for the county offices. The role granted her a cubicle and a tidy income that kept any financial worries at bay. Life seemed steady. Soon the threads of interest dissolved as she became engrossed in filing systems and index cards. A mundane routine took over once again, but it didn't stop her looking for the stories. Her search was never active, not anymore, but her eyes scanned rolling newsreels for the signifiers, keywords that sparked a jolt of exhilaration in her chest, catching her breath for a second.

"Have you called the garage?" Nat nudged her arm with his foot.

She opened one eye.

"No, no I thought you had."

He looked irritated. He pulled his phone from his pocket, checking the screen. "No signal," he muttered, to no one in particular.

Greta stared at him.

He laid back down holding the phone up to the sky. "Shit," he said, then repeated it. "Shit. This place is far out Greta."

"You're telling me," she thought, but it wasn't her who'd insisted on this sodding trip. This was his car, his petrol, his fantasy of the coast. He had wanted to see the place she grew up in; she, on the other hand, had possessed no desire to return here. She shrugged some vague, non-verbal sign of agreement and hugged her legs up to her chest. The skin on her knees was blistering now, white bubbles puckering the tops of her shins, traces of fluid visible just below the surface. The heat made her bitterness visceral, her temper short.

She sighed and levered herself off the bonnet, landing on the soles of her feet. She felt the hot tarmac hiss against her skin. Cramming her feet into her trainers she started off down the road, legs swollen scarlet under the setting sun.

"Hey, hey where are you going?"

His voice was barely a whisper in the dusk. She was already a hundred yards away, pacing quickly.

"Phone!" She yelled, gesturing her hand to her ear in some vague charade of an explanation. He replied but the words got lost in the empty air. She raised her hand as if she had heard, acknowledging whatever he had meant with a flippant wave, half jogging through the dust.

She had been heading for the satellite phone in the lay-by just along the way. She was less than a hundred meters from it now, the name of a local garage scribbled on a shred of paper in her purse. She reached for it, looking back at the car, the road, and Nat. He was spread-eagled on the bonnet, a Promethean sacrifice atop the scratched Skoda.

Her hand was on the phone box now, eyes still fixed on Nat's thin legs, amber in the fading light. She thought of the cottage with its pale blue curtains and three wooden model boats that lined the bay window. She cast her mind to the pre-cooked chicken, packaged and piled on the shelves of the fridge, and the foil-sealed milk on the front step, warm from the day's heat.

Nat's head was still craned back towards the emerging stars, hands tucked at the crest of his skull, cradling it. Greta glanced at her feet. The adder was back; or perhaps it was a different one. The possible symmetry of the moment made her inclined to believe it was the same one that had scouted the edge of the bumper earlier. She was a sucker for fate. She watched it disappear between her splayed feet and into the dry grass verge, its tail vanishing beneath the yellow flowers of a gorse bush. The day was draining quickly from the sky now, fading into blackness. She dropped the phone number, crumpled, at her toes. The wind was silent, anything dropped now was bound to stay motionless; this would be her note.

Then she turned, running before her mind had registered the action. She sprinted like a child, letting the acid rise in her calves and her lungs burn till her vision blurred. She ran and ran and ran, ignoring her name ringing in the soft air behind her. She ran until her body dissolved in the purple dusk.

THE ANNIVERSARY

Barbara Murray

No one in his right mind would have ventured up the fog-shrouded hillside on that Friday morning. But it was the first anniversary of the last climb Gareth and Cerys had made with their sheepdog Ty to do the final check on the lambs before the autumn market. They'd savoured the autumnal reds and golds reverberating around the vivid, sunlit valleys as they trekked up and onto the moors high above the pastures of Pantglas Farm.

So Gareth and Ty were going up that hill, come fog, hell, or high water.

Gareth wanted everything arranged precisely as it had been that morning with Cerys. He wore the same tattered old grey overcoat, borrowed from Dadi years ago. His flat cap and muffler were set firmly in place, just as Cerys had done with them on his last birthday. He double-checked his old deerskin gloves were tucked into his left-hand pocket, primed to protect against the wrong kind of dirt. Cerys's hanky nestled in his right-hand pocket, wrapped carefully around a Rich Tea biscuit she would have given the dog when they stopped for their rest. After, she'd used it to cradle and protect a marsh orchid she'd spotted, intending to press and arrange it.

"You know I don't approve of spoiling a working dog," Gareth grumbled every time Cerys had tossed the eager dog his treat.

"Nonsense! It's you that's got him soft," she'd mocked him in reply.

Gareth was grateful that the persistent thrum of a whole week's ceaseless, torrential rain had finally stopped. An oppressive, windless fog had descended overnight, lending an uncanny stillness to the air. Curtains of the purgatorial mist stole the shapes and forms of man and dog as they set off, and they soon became invisible to each other.

"Come by," Gareth said. The dog advanced at first no more than a few yards, then retreated to place his wet nose in Gareth's extended hand. They moved as a unit. Gareth concentrated on where and how to put his feet whilst Ty assessed the best trajectory for a blind ascent up to the flock. Soon, Ty set Gareth onto the familiar heather-lined sheep track that wove across the top fields, through the tree line and then up further, on to the moors.

Eyes down, Gareth ruminated on what would become of the farm if their son Clifford, now ten, didn't start to show some real interest in its ways and rhythms. The throaty gargling of ewes calling to locate their lambs in the brume caught his attention. Their juvenile, squeaky replies prompted Gareth's attention to shift onto next week's Fat Lamb sales, and he felt a wave of guilt rising in his gorge, that these lambs' days were already numbered.

"That's farming for you." Cerys always said. But tough as it was, Gareth was born to farming and wanted no other life. How could Clifford not want the same? Made no sense to Gareth.

Death was the sharp end of the business, and also of life, Gareth had learned. Farms were dangerous places. Accidents happened and animals got sick. But the Foot and Mouth outbreak that hit the valleys just after the war when Gareth was a child had been another matter altogether.

Hiding in the barn loft, Gareth had glimpsed Dadi's stricken face through the blustering ashes rising from the stinking and smoldering pyre of their cremated livestock. Was this the end of them as a farming family? What future was there with no farm?

The next day, Gareth had been inconsolable when a squall of cinders and ashes whirled around the yard and settled onto his face and hands. The gritty dust got onto his skin and into his hair and would not go away no matter how hard he rubbed. The oily smear staining his skin disgusted him. The dead cells of the hounded, massacred beasts and sheep had permeated his flesh, got into his blood!

Yes, all the farms had been compensated and they'd all started over again. But that, his mother was convinced, had marked the start of his obsessive hand-cleaning and the clamour for certainty which, he was to learn, neither nature nor people could provide.

"Listen," Cerys had clasped Gareth's hand the night before she passed away. "I know the farm means everything to you and your Dadi. But don't you go foisting it onto our Clifford. Let him spread his own wings, won't you? Promise me that, Gareth."

Ty's wet nose brought Gareth back to himself and their business on the hillside. Soon, he could glimpse vague shadows of the flock, still as statues, mist droplets glistening on their ragged fleeces. He was heartened when they arrived at the old sycamore log. It marked the edge of an ancient, rock-strewn copse where Cerys and he had always enjoyed their flask of tea and cake.

By implicit consent, he and Cerys had always kept their eyes front, never regarding the Coal Board's slag tips atop their hill as part of the view. Except for when there was heavy snow. Then, they'd joked about how lucky they were to be living in the Alps! The endless droning whirr of industrial machinery up there was merely the ski lifts!

Gareth loathed those pyramids of mining debris. Why dig out all that filth from the bowels of the earth and haul it up there for all to see on the tops of their glorious hills?

"Dadi's not getting any younger, see?" Gareth said to Ty as the dog wove in and out of the miasma, bossing the sheep. "We'll just have to wait and see how our Clifford turns out, won't we, Ty?" Gareth grumbled. The dog mooched over and sat directly in front of Gareth, locking eyes onto him. He was waiting for his biscuit. "Otherwise, what's it all for, eh?" Gareth said, bringing out the hanky.

To Gareth's surprise, the dog looked away, his head tilting this way and that; he then squinted with full attention at the belt of mist just above, behind which the spoil tips were hidden. The dog's tail shot up and began to quiver. His hackles stiffened as a long, deep growl rolled in his throat.

Unnerved, Gareth took his scruff and pulled the reluctant dog close. "What's spooking you, bach?" he asked, rubbing the dog's head playfully. But Ty pulled away. Gareth strained to hear, testing the air for himself. "It's far too quiet here, Ty. What's happened to the birds this morning?" he asked. "How come these fields aren't more flooded up? Where's all that rain gone?" The dog growled again. "And how come we can't hear the trams and cranes working up there?" Gareth nodded upwards. "Since when did a bit of fog ever stop the march of progress?"

Then came the dreadful rumble, *trwr, trwr,* like a roaring thunder, intense and malicious. Grass trembled around

Gareth's legs, and soon vibrations came up through the ground, rattling the log with Gareth still seated on it. Ty started to bark manically, but was drowned out by the *trwr, trwr, TRWR*.

Next, an earsplitting screech, like chalk on a blackboard, sent the dog scurrying under Gareth's legs.

The thunder's crescendo and its accompanying sudden change in air pressure blasted Gareth's eardrums, leaving him stunned, clutching his ears. On and on the noise went. Odd, and comical it was to have Ty there, barking his heart out, yet seem to be miming!

When the unexpected appears, things happen so fast yet can seem to take forever. *Trwr. TRWR. TRWR...* Surely not an earthquake? In mining country? Never! A landslide, then? Not possible!

Ty nipped Gareth on the calf and snapped him out of the senseless reverie. The dog gripped Gareth's trouser leg in his teeth and pulled him back, away from the log. "Holy hell, *bach*, let's get out of here!" Gareth yelled.

In the rush, his cap flew off and as Gareth lurched for it, Ty twisted round, clamped his jaws onto it and hared away across the field. They made it to a sparse coppice nearby and sunk into the boggy undergrowth. Ty dropped the cap, but as Gareth reached for it, another shrill scream and accompanying abrupt rush of air flattened them both into the cushion of moss and blew the cap away, out of Gareth's stretching reach.

Gareth kept his head down and felt out for Ty to gather him in. Together, they hunkered down with only Gareth's overcoat to shield their backs, shaking and gasping for breath. 'You're bound to find it later Ty,' Gareth reassured himself.

But then Gareth noticed the ashy coal dust swirling above. To forestall his panic, he rummaged in his pocket, only to find the gloves had gone. Even the droning rumble and rush could not distract Gareth from the disgusting sensation of coal dirt on his skin and the familiar pattern to be endured.

As Gareth hauled himself to his knees to retch, he caught sight of the source of the thunderous rumble. A massive lava flow of slurry-grit and tip shale was spilling forth over the land. It was an oozing river, building in momentum, willfully consuming the moorland in its path. The old sycamore picnic log was swept away with no more resistance than a matchstick. Everything in the lava's path added heft and impulsion to the relentless drive and bore of the black mass.

Gareth stood up jerkily and leant against a twisted alder nearby, scanning the scene before him. He took a deep breath. All those heinous sights, all those noxious smells, the explosive, intrusive noises, all of it was coming to him with the most exquisite precision. He noticed his senses expanding to accommodate it all, and that his heart was racing, wild and erratic, intent on escaping up his throat. Desperate to flee, his arms and legs twitched and jerked, yet he was immobilized: doomed to witness the entire horror.

He saw tumbling rocks, flayed tree trunks and splintered fence posts with tendril wires trailing high and wild, all riding the back of the lava's deadly undercurrent. 'All that rainwater has made a river out of the slag tip,' Gareth gasped. He was capable of registering the logical sense of it, but not of envisaging the inevitable consequences.

Together he and the shaking dog waited out an eternity of ten minutes or so, after which Gareth sensed the energy behind the onslaught subside. Then, Gareth girded himself to take stock of the filthy sediment on his skin and clothes. If he could just exert some control over the waves of repulsion about to engulf him, then he would have a better chance of getting away.

His ringing ears were blocked; everything muted. He made several mock-yawns to help unblock them. The vile black dust had filled his ears and plugged his nose. Drossy old coal-bunkers came to mind. His eyes smarted and stung as if barbed wire was stuck in their corners. He flexed his tongue and felt, to his mounting revulsion, that his teeth, his palate and the delicate membranes going all the way down his throat were coated with the same ashy-cindery particles permeating the air. He tried to avoid swallowing, but inevitably it happened. In no time, he was bent double, retching, hawking and spitting over and over, even after his saliva was long depleted.

He sought Cerys's hanky, the biscuit falling away. He daubed the innocent lacy cotton across the clean wet grass where he and Ty had been cowering, then wiped it around his tongue and teeth, spitting out as much of the sulphourous paste as possible. Sweat flooded his brow and trickled down his backbone. With trembling hands, he lifted the quivering dog's head up from where it was tucked under a clamped foreleg and cleared Ty's eyes and mouth. Then he cleaned Cerys's hanky again and braced himself to tackle the dirt stuffing his own nostrils. When he realised he was ramming it further in, he snorted instead, hard, first from one nostril, then the other. He wiped the black snot hanging from his lips as best he could on Dadi's overcoat sleeve then wiped the sleeve repeatedly over the sopping moss.

A silence then descended around them. The fog was lifting. Vivid shafts of light appeared momentarily as a light breeze carried off the remaining veils of mist. Surely the worst was over? Didn't he just have to channel his remaining strength into getting himself and the dog down the hill and home? Then clean up, and the ordeal would be over.

Visibility had improved considerably, but even though Gareth scanned and searched the land, he could see none of the contours and reference points of the hill he knew as well as his own face.

What he did see, not fifty feet away, was the definitive boundary edge of a lusterless black lake. Its ashen mass contrasted ominously with the now vivid sunlight, like freshly brewed tar on a newly surfaced road.

How was it possible he hadn't noticed that before? This dividing line, that started somewhere high in the thinning mist and crept down the hillside toward their land?

As he looked up and down the line, Gareth saw that on the left side of the edge there was the usual shiny bright green of the valley, typically resplendent after a good rainfall; on the right side, it was literally pitch black, obliterated, desolate.

How was he to comprehend such a contrast between the natural and the grotesque?

Why were such malevolent forces, forces he would never understand nor be able to protect and defend himself against, once again violating all he held dear?

The plaintive bleating of the ewes and lambs, panicky and urgent, brought Gareth back into his farmer's instincts. 'The lambs! Ty, the lambs!' he yelled. Ty was already at the swelling black line where the sheep were gathered. Amidst the chaos, lambs and their mothers had been split up. Some of them were gone, smothered in the slag lake. Gareth watched, agape, as these desperate mothers found the courage to nose and prod the intimidating edge, then recoiled from it, only to go back again and again. Such naked loss broke his farmer's heart.

Those on the wrong side of the death line had been sucked away in the black slurry. Those on the right side of the death line had survived. Simple as that, it was. How does that work? Who decides which side of the line anyone ends up on?

How can loved ones be here with you in one ordinary, everyday moment, and then gone the next?

When Gareth saw that Ty was fixating on some lambs still clambering in the sludge, he froze, horrified. With one hand clamping Cerys's hanky over his mouth and nose, he stretched out toward the dog, but had to watch, helpless, as Ty clawed, flailed and scrabbled his way across to the barely alive, exhausted lambs. But the weight and acidity of the slurry soon overwhelmed the dog, forcing him back on his haunches to lick and bite at his lacerated paws. Ty's muzzle had become fouled up, tacking his jaws together. Soon, the dog gave up chafing and resumed his frantic digging.

It took some moments for these observations to settle before Gareth's body took over from his mind. In the time it took him to stagger through the demented sheep to the black edge, Gareth realised that Ty had scuttled atop the slurry's surface and was now in the flow, furiously digging. He'd managed to forge a shallow hollow and was trying to keep the seepage at bay.

He'd got to a lamb's body. Gareth saw a skinned foreleg sticking out at a very wrong angle, the proud flesh and shiny tendons hanging off the bone near the elbow. Ty jawed down onto the leg and hauled back. "No! Leave it Ty!" Gareth shouted, but still the dog kept trying.

Such was the drag of the viscous slurry that Ty couldn't move the lamb, not an inch. No matter how hard he tried. No matter how long he kept at it. What *had* moved, Gareth noted, as a broken branch sailed by, was the dog. Ty had by now drifted about ten feet downstream.

The prospect of losing Ty sent a pulse of dread through Gareth's veins. It weakened his knees and took the breath out of him. The dog gave a final howl of pure anguish before plunging in with a momentous last attempt to seize the lamb. "Ty, no. NO!" Gareth yelled. Gareth could only helplessly watch his old companion choking, retching, digging and howling, driven to his limits by his innate compulsion to retrieve the lamb.

When the dog's exhausted heart could pump no more, Ty collapsed, lifeless, into the lava. The sheep around Gareth began to scatter, leaving him spinning, giddy and winded, until he sunk up to his knees in the mire churned by the panicked sheep.

Gareth's face was then no more than inches away from the still pulsing edge of the black slurry. Sensing the menacing energy of unfinished business contained within, he was forced to inhale the volatile creosote and coal dust leaching from it. The last thing he saw as the acrid fumes overcame him was that the morning sun had finally revealed a sky just as clear and beautiful as the one they'd had this time last year when Cerys was up there with him for the last time.

*

67

Coming to, moments after, Gareth felt a primal surge of indignation flooding his blood and guts. No way was Ty to be taken from him! He may still be saved. He had to be cleaned. Fat lamb market was next week. None of these thoughts registered in Gareth's mind in any concrete way; rather they were just fragments flitting around. Some of them encouraged a deeper breath to be taken, others forced the pupils of his eyes to widen, to soften the scene around him as he took more of it in, and to mobilize him from the stupor poised to overtake him.

Gareth waded into the slurry. To forestall his disgust, he bit down on his tongue and was soon parallel to Ty. He forced his bare hands deep into the oily filth to gain some purchase on the dog's slippery legs and heave him out. Caustic tears burned his eyes, boring two biting channels down his face. As Gareth dragged up the dead dog, the head flopping to and fro, he saw Ty's teeth were still clutching the lamb's leg, now broken off where he had hauled on it that last time.

As the leaden weight of the dog suddenly broke free of the sucking slurry, Gareth wheeled backwards and collapsed on the yielding moss. He hugged and rocked with the dead dog, oblivious to the dirt, filth and grime that now covered his clothes and exposed skin.

Gareth gazed off to distant valleys and rhythmically stroked the dog's head. He tucked the wizened old muzzle snugly into his neck and fondled an ear, just as he had done with him since he was a pup. Spoiling his working dog? Not a bit of it! Yes, Ty had done well. Hadn't he always done well?

"Truth is, see, I hadn't the heart for the lambing. Not this year," Gareth told him. "But you having no lambs to boss about the place would have broken your heart, wouldn't it

68

Ty?" Gareth felt down the length of the dog's spine and gathered up his tail. It pleased him to see that its tip was still clean and white. Somehow, this detail helped Gareth to lay Ty gently on his side, and get to his own feet.

"Our lad Clifford's a book boy, see?" Gareth resumed his conversation with the dog. "Smart lad. Popular. Headmistress says he'll get to the grammar no problem. Go up in the world. Cerys saw that in him, too."

Gareth's gaze drifted up to the summit, away from the horror at his feet. But things were not right up there either.

"Why's that crane toppled over to a funny angle?" he said.

Gareth saw the gap where one of the massive slag piles should have been.

He didn't want to look down. Only when he felt he absolutely must, did Gareth force his gaze downwards, following the course set by that new green-black plumb-line.

Images and impressions simply passed through Gareth's awareness as concepts. There was no need to dwell on anything specific right now, was there? Over by the high end of the top pasture, the forelegs of a dead cow stuck out of the black slurry, its head turned up and back on itself. On instinct, Gareth narrowed his eyes and sharpened his focus onto the lifeless grey eyeball far away. He'd have to report the lost livestock over dinner later, when he and Dadi exchanged the news of the day. But then the vast array of randomly scattered beasts' legs and heads sticking up came into focus.

How had he not seen those before?

That's Dadi's milking herd gone, then.

Further down, the family farm's dwellings and barns were nowhere to be seen.

Gareth looked away, taking in the fresh blue morning sky where the sun blinded him momentarily. When he eventually looked back, retinal sun-spots danced on the black lake where the little artery that connected Pantglas Farm to Aberfan village ought to have been.

Gareth would remember none of what followed.

He gazed away across the valley, where the bright morning sun highlighted the homes and businesses of people on a normal Friday morning. He looked at his filthy boots. How sturdily the cleansing wet turf here gripped his boot treads, held him in place!

He snapped his fingers, expecting Ty's wet muzzle to be there instantly. That strange absence of his constant companion connected, like a synapse, the anguish Gareth had been holding onto since Cerys's diagnosis not six months earlier with the morning's sudden extinction of the lives and land that defined the meaning and worth of his life.

Gareth twisted round and sunk to his knees, the breath escaping from him in a husked roar. His gaze passed over the ravaged land that until today stood for the graft of generations past and the promise of those to come. The venerable oak tree, now no more than a ghost, stood next to his submerged farmhouse. Several darkened beams stuck out of the slurry like the ribs of a scavenged carcass. They were still attached to the gable end of the vanished old barn Dadi had been preparing for overwintering the beasts.

Gareth tried to stand, but couldn't. He began to tremble violently, his jaw locked closed. He clenched his fists into rigid knots, holding them together against his eyes. His ragged nails slit through his palms, eventually piercing the soft muscle beneath. Soothing rivulets of blood trickled down his wrists

70

and disappeared up the raincoat sleeves. Yes, let the pure essence of all those beasts, all the sheep and those precious dogs, and of everyone who had been sacrificed just for being part of him - let them pulse free, away! Eventually, he let himself sink onto the mossy turf.

His head came to rest next to a crumple-stemmed fern. The russety fronds of the summer's fiddlehead were still intact and elegantly feathered. He stretched out an arm and touched it, found it enjoyably pliable and responsive as it furled and unfurled round his blood-stained finger. He sought out Cerys's hanky, which, through some instinct amidst the chaos, he had tucked between his vest and his trouser waistband.

His flittering hand grasped the stem of the fern and plucked it away. He laid it gently on one half of the now ragged and soiled hanky, pressed and covered it with what was left of the other half, and swaddled it away, next to his chest. Another one for Cerys's collection.

The 21st October 2016 was the 50th Anniversary of the tragedy of Aberfan, South Wales, UK. At 09.15 on that day, 144 lives were lost including 116 children, when an unstable mound or tip containing thousands of tonnes of rock-slurry, coalmine waste and tailings, stored on the hill above the town, fell like a landslide onto the village of Aberfan. The falling lake of filth first engulfed a local farm, then a village street, and finally settled on the classrooms and playgrounds of Pantglas school. It was the worst tragedy in recent Welsh history.

THE COASTAL ROAD

Joanne Preston

I don't really know why I get in the car. Actually, that's a lie. I know why. Time is short. I don't really have to think about it for more than a few seconds. The blindfold is passed to me while Aidan has his other hand on the wheel. I will have to tie it myself. Aidan hesitates slightly, but he passes it to me all the same. I know why. It's the same reason I take it without comment. The others made him promise; he'll have trouble if he doesn't. I mustn't see the way there, because then I will guess. It is supposed to be a secret. For now. Most things can be waited for. Most things have to be. Where are we going? Sorry. That comes later. I have to tell another part first.

I smell the air and know we are taking the coastal road. People like to say things are in their blood, don't they? They mean it is part of who they are. Well, the sea is in mine. Along with all the other stuff, the bad stuff. I feel each change of speed, each twist and turn. I both love and hate this stretch of road, significant to me in all the ways that matter.

Every now and then Aidan glances over at me and takes a breath as if to speak. But every time, the actual words fail to come out. Good job I can handle suspense. Frustrated, he turns back to the road until the next time. How do I know he's looking at me, I hear you ask? I know because this is pretty much all he does now. He watches me. He waits. Dreading yet expecting any sudden quick inhalations of breath. I'm not sure if he knows that I know. The blindfold is actually a blessing to him right now. It means he can scrutinize me mercilessly without explanation.

It's funny, despite their apparent need to watch me closely, they also don't like any stark reminders. They watch to make sure that there's nothing to see. Then we can all forget. I can't forget though. Every morning I have to remember. Every morning I go quietly and calmly to the bathroom after breakfast to take between three and eleven. My dream is to take just one. If I take them before breakfast I'm usually sick. Learning curves. The others appreciate this distance of a closed bathroom door. Out of sight . . .etc. If I do this, then for the rest of the day I am relatively free. It always amuses me when the neat, new boxes come every month. Only a month at a time, I am allowed no more. Just in case. What a silly rule. Oh the damage I could do with that twenty-eight if I wanted to. I still have some power. Perhaps they think it is an attempt at optimism as well as being responsible? One month at a time: then you can pretend it's only for twenty-eight days. Twenty-eight days isn't a lifetime though, is it? And a lifetime is what I have been told.

My turn now. I glance over at Aidan. I can see his frown. Blindfold? Again, I don't need to see it to know it's there. I sense his reservations about tonight, but surely we are almost there now? Harriet must have arrived already. Do I blame myself about Aidan and Harriet? His damaged love. How can I? I didn't ask for any of it. He would have done all he has done whatever the cost. It is his way. If anyone was to take charge it was going to be him. He would have seen it as his right. I don't think I ever would have escaped that, even if it hadn't happened. I sit and think. What would I do if he spun the car around? Right now. Started racing in the opposite direction. At this speed I would be knocked against the side of the car; I would bang my head. But after that? I might just laugh. He wouldn't approve; he wouldn't see the funny side. It's been a while since we laughed together. It's been a while since he's made me laugh like he used to. I still understand how he works. But me? No. I don't think he does anymore.

I shouldn't be so light about it. He spent twenty-one years learning about me, and then lost it all. He was presented with a stranger: he couldn't see anything in me except all he hoped I still was; and I tried to give it to him for a while. I really did. I hadn't realised the depths of the changes myself. Once I did, I had to be who I'd become. Who I always would have become? Well, we'll never know.

I was brought to him at the age of one. It is a story that has become a family legend. He was told I was a wonderful gift, and he should take great care of me. The legend says that he absorbed this information silently; he looked at me and then, with almost no hesitation, picked me up and carried me into the house. From that moment it was settled as far as he was concerned. I was a promise made. A certainty he never thought to question. I am suddenly knocked by a wave of tenderness towards him. Blindfolded I reach my hand out and find his left; it is resting near the gears as it always is on this road. He clears his throat at my touch.

"Nearly there Kim." He says.

I move my hand away. He was lost in thought; I interrupted without invitation. And now, he is all too aware of the present again. Brought back before he was ready. I know that feeling all too well.

Eventually we slow down. We must be here. We stop. He sighs. He pulls the keys out of the ignition.

"Kim..." He pauses. I wait. "You look pretty tonight."

Is that a bad thing? He makes it sound like a bad thing.

74

"Thanks." I say, still blindfolded.

Aidan slams his car door a little too enthusiastically. Then he is opening my door and taking hold of my hands to pull me out. We start to walk. He holds my hand to keep me steady. I hear muffled voices ahead: laughter, and excitement. His hand on mine tightens. I feel the outside become the inside; the voices become closer and greater in number. I can hear a few muffled instructions: I am guided; I am positioned; and then I am let go. There is a moment; one moment when I hear nothing and see nothing. I feel utterly alone; it is not unwelcome. Everything has stopped: the quiet, the stillness, is beautiful. I almost want to tear off my blindfold and find myself the last person on earth. Almost.

And then...

"Surprise!"

Shouts. Colour. Singing. Heat from the candles.

They all look at me expectantly. They are desperate for me to mirror their smiles. Not a cheap version of it, but the real thing. They want me to fit back in again, as if I had never become undone. I don't know how to do that. Even if I wanted to. Which I'm not sure I do. I feel like a shadow that doesn't fit. I should be a perfect copy with nothing out of sync. We can all see that I'm not. The smiles are the worst thing about this: the smiles are their hopes, radiating out to me. What can I do? It is becoming uncomfortably clear; in a moment I won't be able to save it. So I blow out the candles and smile. Good girl. Job done.

I start to move through the crowd. People pause their conversations as I pass. They say "hi"; most reach out to touch me on my arms or shoulders. Why do they do this? Is it to

75

check that I'm real? Is it to give comfort? Sympathy? It could be any, or none of these reasons. Before it happened you wouldn't have been able to tell me apart from anyone else here. I would have been mingling, making small talk, helping with planning, choosing the music; and dancing. I loved parties. And now? Now I see a hollowness I didn't before. But one thing hasn't changed. I feel the need to dance; I go anywhere where I can dance. Mostly to places I wouldn't have gone before. Dancing; I always loved it, but now it gives me a release that not much else does. I lose my troubles in the beats of the music: in the words, and the way my body can move again.

Luke blocks my path through the room. I was heading outside to the pool area, to fresh air and space. My host's face is so full of questions he can barely contain himself.

"Kim! So happy to see you! You look well! I mean, *really really* good."

He's not wrong. I looked at myself hard in the mirror before I came tonight. I looked…normal. No outward trace or sign. Except those only I can see. I see the person I used to be sometimes too. Before… She passes me in familiar places, this house, these friends and she should be here tonight. She is often walking the other way as she passes me: she is walking to a life I know nothing about, though on my dark days I speculate sometimes. Why do I know nothing about it? Because it never happened. That is the funny thing about what happened to me. It didn't ask for my life, not in the end. However, if it was going to give me life at all, it was going to be very different. It forced me to see myself, and see the life I might have had. I had to make decisions, choose. That girl. She never stood a chance against herself as she is now. Against me. I am completely changed, and therefore, so forever is she. What I see in those moments when they come is not real. She doesn't exist anymore. I do.

It takes me over an hour to work my way through the sea of people before I can make it outside. Every time a conversation ends, someone is waiting in the wings to start another. I move perhaps a few steps every twenty minutes. I can't remember how many times my drink is refilled. I phase in and out as I repeat myself endlessly. Endless too is the question, "What happened?" What happened? They ask me like they don't know. It's really very simple. And so I tell them. Again, and again.

I listen for each new song on the party playlist someone has thrown together. My need for some sense of release is getting stronger. I know Aidan has been watching me from across the room all night. I ignore him. I can handle this. I can handle myself. Before, I used to be the one to drag him to parties. I wanted him to meet the people in my life. He always impressed them. He was a real grownup, the rest of us only pretenders. Ten years will do that I guess. He would always appear at my side and pull my hand discreetly when he'd had enough. It was our secret signal that my ride was leaving. I would say goodbye, drain my glass, and suppress a smile. I never pushed him too far. After all, it was impressive. Not many others like him would have been so involved in my life: where I went, who I knew, and what I liked to do. He always was. If that was being protective then, what should I call what he's doing now?

The fresh air outside is welcome. I let it wash over me. The pool is centre stage; everyone around it forms an inattentive audience. I gaze at the aqua blue water; I am mesmerized. At last, a song I like comes on. This one is on my personal playlist at the moment. The one I distract myself with as I present my arm so they can check my blood. Less frequent now than it used to be, but still more often than I would like. I close my eyes briefly. I let the song carry me away and before I know it I am in the water. I am swimming lengths down the pool. The water is beautifully cool. The air is close and muggy tonight; it is a heat that envelops you and drains all energy. I revel in the smooth texture of the water on my skin. I am swimming fast and far, leaving it all behind. Before I reach the other side, I stop and stand up. I feel exhilarated, as if I just swam the length of the sea, coast to coast. It can't have been more than 10 metres.

Suddenly, a gasp. A cry. I don't know who from. I turn and look at everyone. I am still smiling triumphantly, I think. I can still hear the music but no one is talking. The silence finally reaches me and I realise I have a rapt audience. I wade to the end of the pool. I pull myself up to sit on the edge. I am wet but not cold. Gabriella, my other host, approaches me. She bends down in her heels and asks if I'm okay.

I reply without hesitation. "Could you get me a drink? I seem to have lost mine."

This is the very last thing she expects me to say, and it does the trick. She is caught so off guard she smiles by habit.

She straightens and says, "Of course."

As she turns to go, there is an almost visible wave of relief that ripples through the crowd; they return to their conversations gradually. She walks back towards the house. Everyone realises there is no impending crisis and I even hear a few chuckles of laughter in amongst the noise. Now that they feel allowed to see the funny side. What just happened for me was a beautiful moment. I take a minute.

Gabriella is working her way back to me. I watch her weave through the crowd. Before she gets to me, someone stands in front of her, barring her way. He has his back to me. From this view I decide I don't know him. Whatever he is saying, Gabriella is considering it carefully. She glances at me; she is wavering, hesitant and unsure. I don't really feel those things anymore, and so I watch interested. Finally, she seems to have been convinced. She hands the guy the drink she was bringing to me and walks back to her other guests. I decide that he has presumed something long before he turns round and meets my eye.

He sits down at the side of the pool next to me. Smiles are powerful, and can be bestowed as gifts. I decline to be generous so quickly. The lights seem to recede a little, atmospheric you might say. I guess what we will talk about will be significant. I wait for his first line. I can tell a lot by the opening line. I don't know if people know how revealing it is. Perhaps, I should tell them at some point?

"So what happened?" He asks.

Predictable. Too easy. I inwardly sigh and press play on the pre-recording. No need to be unsociable, even if I am somewhat disappointed...

"No." He says, stopping me in mid flow.

What does he mean "no"? This is the story people want. I know that.

He smiles and says again, "No. I mean, tell me what really happened."

I don't say anything. I think I just frown.

79

He continues, "You don't think I can tell that's not really what you're thinking? You've told it so many times you know it backwards and forwards. Am I right? You've got it word perfect."

I still don't say anything. My turn to be wavering, hesitant and unsure. I'm not giving anything away yet.

He speaks again, "Look, I'm not pretending to be a mind reader... but you look like what's going on in your head is a lot more interesting than what they've all been saying... and I've heard a lot of things about you. I want to know what really happened. How you felt. What you saw. What you feel like now, and what you are going to do next. So would you tell me what really happened?"

Who is this guy?

A thought slowly dawns on me; he could be one of THOSE. They like all the terrible details; they like to feel scared by what you say, appalled even. Then they go back to their lives convinced that it could, or should, never happen to them. I decide to test him.

"Some things can't be unshared you know. Some things stay with you. A confidence... you hold it for the rest of your life. Can you do that?"

He thinks for a moment. "I don't know. I think so."

I allow myself a small smile. I think. Will I regret this tomorrow? And then I do it. I tell him. Everything. I wing it; I go completely off script. Each sentence is new and not thought through. It keeps my attention. I decide I could get used to this.

Is it wrong for me to admit I enjoy each reaction that flits across his face? The flinches, the raised eyebrow of surprise quickly contained, and the steady gaze that is calm and yet cannot completely control the sympathy, even sorrow, that flashes in his eyes. I don't leave anything out. No sugar coating. Not this time. It's raw and uncomfortable. As it was for me. I find myself experiencing some strange disconnect: to speak it out like this I have to speak as if it happened to someone else. To remember that it happened to me, to remember how it all felt, is too much. And yet, it wasn't too much! I am still here. The human capacity for pain is surprising. There are a few words I don't speak; there are a few names of procedures that, even now, make me dig my nails into the soft palms of my hands to control the feeling of panic. I don't spare him much. I get the impression he realises this too.

I stop. I expect an almighty silence or, at most, a practised expression of regret. He takes my hand before I have any thought to stop him. He kisses my hand and then holds it between his.

He simply says, "I'm sorry."

It's not been said like this before. This time it means something. He looks at me. I feel something tight inside of me; something that I have closed off; something I have refused to own or open; and it releases and gives way. I feel the relief of it and marvel. I didn't know how tight I had closed it off until now. I am almost angry at his discovery of it and yet, I am not. It is open now and it bleeds slowly into every part of me. It is surprisingly bearable, even okay, even good. With the same determination and certainty I seem to have woken up with since it happened I don't hesitate when I say, "I don't want to be here."

He hears me and smiles.

"Let's go." He says, pulling me to my feet.

If people are watching I am unaware. Sometimes it's good to be unaware. I don't even glance around to see if Aidan is watching us leave. We pass Harriet and I stop quickly. She looks confused: at my smile, and at the guy holding my hand and waiting calmly for me to follow him. Harriet looks at me.

"I'm okay. Tell him." I say to Harriet.

I wait to see that she has understood me. I wait until the acceptance crosses her face: the constant watching is breaking us all. She smiles just a little and nods. Only then do I feel I can leave. I am not immune. I know the care directed at me, at least where Aidan is concerned. I am doing this for him; I am doing this for me.

Driving away feels more like driving towards something. Back along the coastal road. No blindfold this time. I watch everything. He drives confident of the road; I sit confident in him. There is much more to say but we don't speak yet. We enjoy the moments first. What began at the pool side is continued. In the silence I remember what really happened. It is the version of events that only I used to know. I see it all in front of me, but funnily its effect on me has changed. I see it all clearly, but it doesn't stick to me as it once did. For the first time I can imagine something beyond it. He turns to smile at me. I smile back and let the memories come. This time it's different.

I was twenty-two when I fell backwards off a cliff. I just about managed to put myself back together again at the bottom. I'm talking metaphorically. Naturally. It wasn't an actual cliff. Although to be fair, it might have as well have been. The end result was very nearly the same. I, of course, never was. Afterwards I started to dream: I dreamt of silver and white; I dreamt of syringes; and the closely monitored pressure of my blood. I remember nail vanish and braids in my hair. The long list of promises I made to myself, but didn't actually write down. Lying on that table I heard them. I still remember.

"Okay Kim, I want you to breathe in for me. Long, deep breaths. Your eyes will close in a moment. We've got you. You'll be back with us before you know it…"

She never did come back. I opened my eyes three and a half hours later. I felt perhaps I was less. I felt that for a while. But I have changed my mind. Now I am starting to think I am not less, but more. And, now you know. Now I am ready to let everyone know. What happened to me happened. But there is more.

I don't know where we are driving. I suspect this beginning is not just a ride home. Perhaps we will drive and talk, perhaps we will go for a drink and, perhaps, we will dance. For the moment at least, it doesn't matter. There is more. And *that* is what matters.

THE CAVE

Stephen Edward Reid

It was a dark and balmy night (weren't they all?) upon the Island, as Naigraid Horner sat naked on the sand looking out into the vast beyond. With the wind rustling through his wiry thinning hair and the sea spray of the waves caressing his legs, he began to wonder if maybe he should go inside. Lost in the heaving sounds of crashing waves, he failed to notice the soft footsteps behind him as Bolly Longstaff approached. Bolly took a seat next to Naigraid and pulled his canvas blanket around his body to shelter himself from the breeze.

"Are you not cold?" asked Bolly.

Naigraid considered the question then shrugged, dismissing it entirely. "No," he thought to himself, "I'm not. Obviously. Otherwise I'd be covered up. Or inside."

"I thought I heard the sound of a young lady singing just now," said Bolly.

"Was she any good?" asked Naigraid.

"I think you may be missing the point, Captain."

But he wasn't missing the point. He understood that Bolly was suggesting that there was another person on the island. But there wasn't. There was just the two of them and it had been that way for four months. There wasn't an inch of the island they hadn't checked. Except the cave.

"I was thinking," begun Bolly, tentatively, "that we could maybe check the cave."

"Just in case there's a singer in there?"

"Just in case…." Bolly wanted to choose his words carefully, "there's *anything* in there."

Naigraid silently stared out towards the black night, calming himself with the controlled breathing exercises he had taught himself many years previously to cope with mounting stress levels.

"Naigraid?" Bolly waited for an answer.

"Was she any good? This singer?" eventually came the response.

"She was all right," was all Bolly could think to offer in way of a critique.

Naigraid let out a long drawn out breath and slowly rose to his feet, arching his back and stretching his arms out. He felt old. He stalked off back towards their camp, uttering a promise that they would wait "until morning."

"Until morning then," agreed Bolly, already imagining how wizard it would be to see a lady on their island.

***

Bolly often thought of the shipwreck. He replayed the events over and over in his head in a compulsive way, night after night, almost as if he could somehow alter what had happened through sheer force of will. Naigraid never spoke of it and became quite irritable if it ever came up during conversation. But Bolly thought of little else. Once, just once, Naigraid had opened up and spoken of the tragedy but he maintained that most of the terrible events of that night were stricken from his memory. He had told Bolly that all he had remembered was a feeling of falling, as if jumping from a great height and awakening on an island. Bolly, on the other hand, could recall the entire event, from the initial impact of the object from the sky right up until the moment they arrived upon their new home. He had been replaying the event through his mind in an attempt to work out if he had first injured his foot upon the lifeboat or the rocks surrounding the island when his Captain, Naigraid, awoke with a loud expulsion of air. Naigraid was a phenomenal morning person, never failing to instantly rise to his feet to begin his day the second he awoke from slumber.

"To the cave," bellowed Naigraid, hoisting his naked body upwards.

"Did you not want some breakfast first?" But Naigraid was off. Bolly hastily put on his trousers and what was left of a once fine shirt and scrambled to get his meagre tools and rations together for an exploration. Folding them into his canvas blanket, he tied them to a wooden stick he kept handy and headed off after Naigraid. He quickly caught up with his Captain, falling in slightly behind him and becoming transfixed by his gently wobbling buttocks as he walked. It had always struck Bolly as incredibly strange that his Captain had maintained his healthy weight, whilst he himself had become a shell of his former self, with protruding ribs and gaunt face. They both ate the same food and yet their bodies seemed to function in vastly different ways. Whilst Bolly was lost in his own thoughts, Naigraid turned to look over his shoulder and noted the staring of his once First Mate. "Eyes forward, Bolly", he offered and ambled on.

***

They had been to the cave before but had never gone inside it. Their first exploration around their new home, in which Bolly had drawn a fairly impressive map of the whole island, had had just that one notable omission. Naigraid had called it a frontier that they were not yet ready to conquer. Bolly had happily left it well alone. There was plenty more of the island to explore and their various survival needs didn't offer the luxury of heading into an abyss. As they approached it again, for the second time in four months, they stopped at the same point as they had before, amidst a small growth of a purple flower which neither man could identify. Ahead of them lay the entrance to the, as yet unexplored, cave.

"Do you think anybody could be inside?" offered Bolly optimistically.

"Your singer?" answered Naigraid. "No."

They waited too long, uncomfortably long, just looking at the entrance but remaining rigid.

"Shall we…." began Bolly, hoping his sentence didn't need completing.

Naigraid screwed up his face, standing firm and letting time slowly pass him by. Bolly ran his hands through his full beard, letting the hairs tickle across his fingers in a way he always did when his mind hit upon any tricky decision-making moments.

"I don't think…" began Naigraid, hoping his sentence didn't need completing once more.

"No," agreed Bolly, "maybe you're right."

Naigraid turned, happy with their decision, heading back towards their camp. Bolly, as ever, was not far behind.

***

That night Naigraid lay sleeping, his rampant snoring bludgeoning the night's silence. Bolly lay on his back, eyes open, looking through the cracks in their makeshift home and watching the stars sparkle above him. He had had a home once, with two dogs, a house keeper, cook, gardener and a wife he wasn't particularly fond of. He had suspected that the gardener was a frequent visitor to his wife's chambers but hadn't felt particularly aggrieved enough to pursue these thoughts. He had lived with an opulence granted him by his wealthy father, Shaftesbury Longstaff, the founder of the Longstaff Liveries in the East End of London. But he had always had a hankering for the sea and had stowed away at the first opportunity, experiencing life upon the salty waves through many years that saw him rise from stowaway to First Mate in just fourteen short years. And now, he was lost, stranded upon an island with just one other and imprisoned on all shores by the very ocean he had always sought out. His thoughts were interrupted as Naigraid shifted position, clambering round to rest upon his stomach. Bolly waited for a sign that his friend, his Captain, had awoken, but a brief moment of silence was broken as the snoring continued once more. Bolly's thoughts turned to slumber and he rolled onto his side and closed his weary eyes. It was then that the sound of singing caressed his ears. His eyes opened but he remained still, listening intently. After a moment's contemplation, he gently eased himself to his feet, dressing himself and heading out into the cool night. He cocked his head, almost as if a dog, as he tried to find a source of the soft singing that still sounded. As if in a trance he headed back to the cave.

***

Naigraid awoke, instantly rising to his feet and yawning – one of his great pleasures. His eyes darted around the small

88

makeshift homestead and he noticed the absence of his companion. He headed outside, standing upon the sand and looking around.

"Bolly!" he bellowed. No answer.

"Bolly!" he bellowed. Again.

With an audible 'harrumph' he grabbed his wooden stick and set out to search for his friend. He didn't like waking to anything different. He was a creature of habit and had once ignored Bolly for several days after his friend had relieved himself one morning into the sea rather than upon their usual place behind the camp. "Why spoil the sea you buffoon?" he had chastised him, "we have a whole island here!" But this was different. Bolly was gone. Bolly never went anywhere. Not without him. He began an investigatory search of the island but in his heart he knew exactly where he should look. And yet, he still spent several miles circumnavigating the cave in order to check all possibilities before heading towards the inevitable one. When he arrived before the cave he stopped amidst the purple flowers and looked into the darkness beyond.

"Bolly!" he bellowed. No answer.

"Bolly!" he bellowed. Again.

He raised his foot, as if a step forward were imminent and yet it seemed to hold in the air for the longest time, before it eventually returned to its natural position next to the other one. Naigraid stood still. Why would Bolly have gone into the cave? It seemed preposterous. Especially without him. There must be another answer. He must either be hiding (unlikely, thought Naigraid) or have washed out to sea somehow (probably that, he thought.)

He visited the same spot outside the cave each morning for the next month, each time persuading himself that his friend, his First Mate, Bolly, had washed out to sea. Somehow. Perhaps during a morning swim or a mishap with a wave during a moment of self-celebration. Either way, whatever it may have been, he was sure he hadn't disappeared into the cave. Naigraid was not a man known for his psychoanalytical depth and yet he had given the cave plenty of consideration this past month and had come to what seemed like a natural conclusion. The cave was not for him. The cave emitted a dark radiance, alluring in the most obvious frontier ways but so obviously a trap or a haven of misdeed of some sort. Though seemingly just a cave, Naigraid was almost certain that it was a cave that was not meant for curious eyes. It was a cave to be left well and truly alone and that morning seemed no time to change that.

"Bolly!" he bellowed. No answer.

"Bolly!" he bellowed, but with no answer forthcoming, he burst into a flood of uncontrollable tears.

Naigraid suddenly felt his nakedness, as if God's eyes had disapprovingly fallen upon him. He hadn't cried since he was a child of seven when his angry mother had beaten him with a wooden chair leg for the slightest of misdeeds. He couldn't even recall what he had done but he had felt the pain every time his emotions had risen to the surface ever since. Also he felt it when it got cold. And sometimes in the morning having arisen from a particularly hard night's sleep. He wiped away his tears with the back of his large hands, cursing to himself for being so emotional. He turned his back on the cave. As his body shifted and he prepared to walk away, he was taken by a sound emanating from behind him. From the cave. The sound of a lady singing. Heavily schooled in the works of Homer's Odyssey, Naigraid certainly wasn't about to enter the cave to satisfy his curiosity. No, he would stand firm and resist, heading back to his camp. He would do that soon, he thought. In just a moment. After he had listened for a while and garnered more knowledge of the siren and her song. But no amount of straining could help him decipher words let alone meaning. The answer wasn't standing here amidst the purple flowers at the mouth of the cave. It was within.

***

Naigraid awoke. Back in his camp, under the makeshift roof of the small wooden hut that he and Bolly had constructed from what little shipwreck they had found those five months ago. He had shivered as the night grew colder and the cave's presence summoned him to enter, but he had resisted. He had walked backwards, each careful barefoot step taking him further from the cave. Slowly, steadily, until eventually he had put enough distance between himself and the mouth of madness and he had run, run as fast as he could safely back to what he now called home. There had been more tears, near hysteria, but ultimately he had laid down and sleep had overcome him. He was on his feet with his friend's canvas blanket wrapped around him as he went round to the back of the hut to relieve himself. He no longer saw the island as his. He felt like an intruder and that each new day he spent there meant a day closer to succumbing to the cave. He felt its control expanding out and engulfing the island. And he knew that he must escape. He must head back out to sea – the same sea that had expelled him all those months previously. He would not make a crude raft. He would not build a signal and cry for help. He would swim. Without looking back to survey his camp one last time, he marched forward, letting his blanket fall from his body as he strode into the sea, walking until the waves took his legs and then he swam, briskly and powerfully, straight ahead to salvation.

WE ALL FALL IN LOVE IN AMNESIA, NEBRASKA

Stephen Wade

This is about the day Siggy Hortmann never came back home. Not alive and kicking anyway. Dead in fact. Oh and it's about Hatty Lebarr, whom I love. Notice I said *whom*. I'm the only guy in town who says *whom* and that's kinda cool. She's more adorable than tomato ketchup and fries. Oh and it's really about the kiss that snatched away my soul and made me a slave to love. In fact, it's down to road-kill that I know what love actually is.

Oh, and it's about Chet Two Winds and the love-inducing tale of a Cherokee's affection for an old German. I hope this is making sense to you, because it does all come together eventually.

I was born and still hang around in Amnesia, Nebraska. You know these sleepy places. The town crossroads has a monument with the motto 'Lest we Forget'. But boy that's easy to do around here. There's dust and there's corn. Then there's beer and corn. After that, there's school and the big yellow bus. Then corn. The most action you see is either Rex the mad hobo spitting gobs or Chet Two Winds banging on about herbs and cures picked from the fields. He claims he was born a true Arapaho one hundred and ten years back.

Course, Amnesia is not what you would call a town – more an idea that seemed a good thing at the time but turned out to be twenty houses all in a bad mood. Every family there is good nineteenth century immigrant stock, rumoured to be mostly Germans in search of farmland and one lot, the Dacheronoviches, who set off with a handcart to go West but then Pa was sick after two miles so they came back. The place does that to you – makes you try to escape and then tugs you back.

But I'm dwelling on the good side. There's bad as well. I mean, there's trying to grab some tenderness and affection from the young women. For me, there was just the one that summer; the summer before we all went away to college in Lincoln. She was Hatty Lebarr and she was sex on legs, the goddess of desire, and aching for her was real bad. She only spoke to big guys with legs like redwood trunks.

Now that's where I come in, as my name is Red – well, Jared 'Red' Scharrer. I suppose I'm just two pegs above a geek, though not a pure geek as I can't press the right button on any gizmo.

So back to how we lost Siggy Hortmann. It all happened cos we was wanting to be neighbourly and make a contribution. Siggy was a retired schoolteacher, a true eccentric I suppose, who tended to hang around with Chet Two Winds and jaw about the Great American Novel or some such. Either it was that or the latest shambles perpetrated by the Chicago Cubs. Well, I never would have joined in the fiasco if it hadn't been the case that Hatty was there, and no competition.

Still not making sense am I? That's why I was bound for Lincoln, not some neat East Coast place with old piles of stone to show off. It was all down to Siggy and his need to 'contribute somethin' so he took on the role of boss for the 'Adopt a Highway' scheme. Now if this is new to anyone, let me explain the notion.

The thinking is this. Each good-hearted community in the vast Cornhusker State takes on a stretch of Interstate 80 and takes care of the crap on the highway. Now that seems like a cosy brush and spade number until you reflect that a whole range of what Davy Crockett would have called 'critters' tend to cross that asphalt. Therefore, the poor saps in the sweep-up party find themselves scraping the odd carcass of coyote or wood chuck or rabbit. Even, on occasion, an antelope.

Well, a teenage brain-child would never get involved, right? Unless he had a head full of voices telling him he was the Saviour of the Fallen World or maybe a nutter with a desire to play frizbees with a pizza-shaped fox corpse.

But I heard it on the grapevine that Hatty was doing this for penance, after being a rebel and staying out beyond ten thirty. So, as I was also in disgrace, I offered to help. Siggy gave me the same searching, mistrustful look he had always given me at school. He had always doubted me since the day I blagged my way through a discussion on *The Great Gatsby* and he knew I'd never read it. He kept trying to get me to say the main character was Robert Redford, but I could lie for the Western World and stay cute-faced, man.

Siggy was a tad deranged though. He was so far out he'd lost sight of shore. Course, he was basically German, like most of us around Amnesia. He came from a family of asshole book-learners and was so anal he daren't buy an ice cream until he checked the tub for rat-droppings. That was cos he read a piece in *Scientific American* about the rat scourge. Siggy was terrified of rats. He used to talk about them obsessively. Rumour was he was once bitten by one and that accounted for the red blotch above one eye which he gave out was a birth-mark.

Now, Siggy had a military cast of mind so he drilled us, the road-squad, and he gave instructions as we stood in line fully enveloped in bright orange jackets and leggings, with bands of shiny, trimmed illuminated paint on us, looking like remnants from some legion of the damned in a bad SF movie. There was me; tall, red-haired and dreamy, eyes fixed on Hatty. There was gorgeous Hatty; tall, slim, with shiny black hair and absolutely, totally mesmeric eyes. Then there was Chet Two Winds, wrinkled like a scrotal sack, squinting out of his one good eye, and muttering to himself about the White-Eyes and their no-good medical methods. Finally there was young Oswald Watter, and he was simple. Well, truly he was the type to claim that he had a deep wisdom, and to substantiate that he said wise things. This covered up the fact that he couldn't tell left from right nor count to five.

Oswald's wise things consisted of remarks about the weather. I recall that day he said,

"A cloud trimmed with blue, that's sure-fire tornado."

He was bound to get one right each year, I guess.

"Now, this is not simply a perfunctory thing. This is an honorable duty." Siggy said, as we sat in the Perkins having a coffee before the station-wagon was loaded up and we moved out over the dirt-road to the highway.

"See, when the good folk from Iowa and Illinois come steaming this way, they'll look down at the grass and the concrete and they'll think that at least a few miles of Nebraska was clean enough to sit on with your bare ass." Siggy blushed after saying that, remembering that some ex-students were present.

"No listen up, I'm not sure about this, I mean you White Eyes tend to murder little mammals. Are you gonna ask me to collect a mammal or two?" Chet said.

"Why sure we are. There's road-kill."

"AAAAH . . . Don't say that word . . . It was the same with the buffalo . . ."

"Get him a beer, his nerves are bad." Siggy said.

"When the clouds over the plains go, a wind from heaven kills . . ."

"Shut up, Oswald. You look like Homer Simpson's bad cousin," Hatty said.

I was wondering why the hell I was doing this as the old Dodge thundered its way out of town. I mean, it was unpaid, unclean and like a nightmare. But then Hatty looked around and smiled at me and I knew why I was there. Just to be in her company for three hours would be bliss on a level unknown even to Cathy and Heathcliff. I had to think of something that would make me cool. I know that I said, "Hey, Hatty, you like a coke?" and I put my James Dean creased-face look on before I handed her the bottle, wiping it with the sleeve of my check shirt.

"Okay Red, as you're a gentleman. And by the way, watch out for Two Winds, he's real old. Mom says he's a hundred and twenty."

"That's Cheyenne years," I laughed. And you know, she joined in. She laughed as well, and for a second, she looked right into my eyes – Hatty, the girl who usually looked right through you unless you had biceps wider than your neck and a belly tough as a rubber tyre.

Then came the Interstate. My God it was loud. They were doing some road works on the first stretch, as we drove to our section. There were about five giant diggers roaring and some guy with a voice from Hades yelling at a poor sap who was peeing in a ditch.

"The Corn-Pisser State," Two Winds laughed. When he smiled his black teeth showed, like a row of dead matchsticks.

I noticed that Hatty was the first to spot the wayward driving of old Siggy.

"I'm not being cruel, but you sure you passed the driver-test Mr. Hortmann?"

"Sure. Why you doubtin' me, woman?"

"Well, you're driving down the roadworks lane and there's a guy shouting at you. He says you're a senile old fart-bag if I'm not mistaken."

"What? The bastard! Want me to take him out for you Siggy? I got my gun."

Two Winds produced a rusty old musket.

"No, grab the gun, kids, grab the gun!"

It was the first bad sign that the day was going to turn out wrong somehow. We had to wrestle the old man to the floor, as the Dodge rocked and creaked. After a whole spite of cursing, his bony frame was held down by Oswald's giant butt. In the struggle, I managed a long look at Hatty's gorgeous cheek in the sunlight. It has that magic sort of femininity that sends a message to a guy's knees that they should turn to cardboard. She never saw me. I had dreamed of the day when I could really look at her beauty without being thought perverted. I suddenly knew what the poem really meant – the one about a woman walking in beauty like the night.

The Dodge slammed to a stop. Siggy got out and proclaimed that 'this was our bit' so we should get out and grab some tools.

"Two Winds, you git along there a way and concentrate on beer cans. There's your bag. Oswald and me'll drive to the far end and work back. That leaves the kids to sort the rest." He winked at me.

But I was smiling so my face split. Hatty sort of patted my arm and put a small shovel in my hand. I gave her a brush and some powerful-looking fluid which was supposed to shift tar, so Siggy said, "Now, one crucial thing, you people. You git any difficulties along here, take one of these red flags and wave 'em like hell."

"What?" Two Winds said, puzzled.

"You git trouble, you wave this," Oswald said. I was amazed that he had understood.

"Shit . . . I git trouble I wave this . . ." Two Winds held up his musket.

"Chet, if you try to fire that, we'll be scraping you off the highway, you loony half-breed!" Siggy frothed at the mouth as he did when vexed.

Ten minutes later we were alone, strolling along, meeting the occasional screwed-up bag or old cloth. It was the nearest thing to heaven I'd experienced at that time. I mean, it was building hot – upper nineties I'd say. The road stretched ahead and we were alone. Alone, apart from several thousand vehicles of course, so privacy was going to be tough. Still, like your average young male from the Rockies to the Alaska roof, I tried to entertain.

First I sang. God knows why but I sang 'At Home on the Range' as done by Roy Rogers, a guy who haunts my dark side. This had no effect except a blank stare. Then I tried cool and spoke some lines from a poem. The day was turning into a creative writing project and it was all about Hatty.

'What is this life if, full of care,
We have no time to stand and stare . . .'

You know those soulmate moments? This was one. Hatty turned to me, screwed up her gorgeous eyes and said, 'Hey, one of my favourites. I LOVE that poem. You know the guy who wrote that bummed around here – and he lost a leg."

Then I crapped on the situation. It's what I always do with women. I lose it and go for the dumbo answer. I said, "Did he ever find it?" and then did my Yogi Bear snigger.

Hatty gave me a look that said I was a brainless dork who deserved to get stuck in this two-bit dump.

"You're laughing at me!" She said, and sprinted on ahead, in a mood, till she became just a dot on the horizon. I refused to chase her and apologise. I was too ashamed of myself and I was talking to Norman, my other inner dark self who murders any sexiness I might occasionally have in front of women. Every man has a Norman. Even the coolest dudes around have this Norman geek trailing after them, and there they are, like dark shadows across a sunny day outside a cafe in Italy. The Norman comes and stands over a man, just as the cheesiest lines come out and might just have the tiniest chance of impressing the woman.

That was the turning-point of the day. I sensed that she was shouting. Maybe she was in trouble. She was waving her arms around and screaming. I sprinted to her, ready to take on a tiger if it appeared from the cornfields.

There she was, her mascara smudged by tears, bending over a poor panting hound, just clinging on to life. There was a stream of blood from his mouth and his eyes were not moving. His tail just gently flapped and he gave a low wheeze,

100

trying to communicate. He was a big dark brown mongrel with that tinge of white around the mouth that tells you he's a senior citizen and that crossing a road has become something like tackling the Mojave Desert.

"Red, do something! He's dying!"

"Like what? I ain't even got a plaster!"

"Like tear your shirt sleeve." I looked dumb.

"But he's bleeding from inside!"

"I know, you idiot, but he's got a wound in one leg too, see!"

She had a hand on his back right leg and she was holding a thumb across a wound. The blood had covered her hand.

Then the brain started to function. "I got the flag!" There it was in my back pocket, so I waved it and jumped up and down, yelling for the truck. Saving that dog became my one mission in life. It would bring me closer to the lovely Hatty.

"Hurry up, he's sinking fast, Red," she gasped, pulling at my trousers. That was a step in the right direction.

The flag idea didn't entirely work well. Siggy arrived in the truck, saw the situation, and got to work. Sure. But so did about six other vehicles. Everyone who felt like being a Good Samaritan braked and joined in. Siggy was there, naturally, and I couldn't figure out if he was cool or simply imitating the Living Dead. He seemed to know what to do.

"Poor feller. But the situation's not hopeless. Now, all three of us together, we have to lift him onto the back seat of the truck and I'll get him to some medico."

But the problem was the bunch of strangers all giving advice.

"Poor pooch, be gentle."

"I got some cream here - helps to freeze the blood they say."

"Don't move him. I'm a doctor."

I had to concentrate on Hatty. She was an emotional wreck now. Also, what a wonderful opportunity to make some progress. I left the crowd to attend to the dog, and took Hatty around and down the bank to sit on a fence and just hug her.

"Life is so thin. I mean there was that living creature, enjoying the smells of a summer day, just taking in the greenery and then woooosh, gone. Life is just like a thin piece of paper and it can sort of get wet and sort of - am I making sense Red?"

I was a little lost, but I felt it was right to reassure her and I said that she was making perfect sense and that the best thing was for me to put my arm around her, and she loved that.

There seemed to be a long silent period, with only the distant hubbub of the medical consultation up by the road. Otherwise, I was beginning to feel like a heel, a jerk. I mean, well, I am a guy, and, well to say true, I sort of wandered from the comfort stage to the feeling the bra-strap stage. It could have been the end of everything, but I was saved by the dog.

The moment her tear-filled eyes looked at me with a budding accusation of being a pervert, not a reconstructed male, there was one hell of a loud cheer. The dog had got to its feet and walked. In fact it walked off into the grass as if there had been no more than a slight bop from a strong wind.

The crowd dispersed. Vehicles were on the move again. I saw Siggy stare at us and so we moved back into action.

Two Winds had been panting along, slowly coming to see what the fuss was all about. When he arrived he was breathless and had to sit down on a rock.

"All for nothing! I came to administer some Black Fever leaves but I see the damned thing just walked off! Well, here they are. I had to root around in all kinds of shit to find these."

I had to show an interest so I asked about these grubby things.

"These is magic for anything - gout, the farts, gut-pains, lumbago, shivering grimbles - it sorts 'em all out. Yessir, Black Fever leaves. You only find 'em growing near wood-chuck shit. Hence the questionable aroma around old Chet at this moment."

"Hold on, say nothing else, I want to know about this grimbles," Hatty said.

"Oh, ain't nothing for a young female to worry about, less of course you're getting bad women's pains at the time of the cycle."

She blushed.

"Chet, she just wants to know about the things," I said.

"Well now, you just rub these leaves on the painful bit just below the spot where you git the grimbles, drink a whole lot of water and sit still for a while. Works a treat. Now you see, I've given you an old Cherokee secret. It was knowledge told to me by Hair Smells Bad one dark night in the wilderness."

"Yes, but Mr. Two Winds, what ARE the grimbles?"

"You mean you don't know? Women, the grimbles shuts down the whole sexual and emotional system."

I don't want to seem callous, but I nudged Hatty along and we left him to one of his monologues.

It must have been half an hour later when the real panic set in. Course, being Amnesia, it was preceded by a farce. This was in the shape of Hatty's grandma arriving with a picnic. She arrived in second gear and in fact usually drove everywhere in second gear, though she never went beyond the two square miles around her home. Now although she arrived with a neat traditional basket, even covered with a red and white check gingham cloth, the cats ruined the occasion.

See, Grandma Dacheronovich, 'Dash' for short, is sane, but only by the definition of the year BCE 400. It all stems from her penchant for cats. So here's this old Chevvy loaded up with ice cream, bagels and cream cheese, flasks of coffee and boxes of muffins. Also liberally stacked with her own cherries and raspberries from the garden but then, the moggies are crawling all over the stuff.

"Fine now you young folk, get some chuck. Git off that, Sidney! Darn, Sidney licked the ice cream. The lid slipped. Still, cats have clean tongues you know. Send for the others, young Red."

I almost made the mistake of waving the lousy flag again, but thought better, and luckily Two Winds was within hollering distance, so he passed the invitation on to Oswald, and hopefully then to Siggy.

I was wrong.

We were sitting on this stinky old rug Grandma Dash spread out, trying to avoid biting anything delicate, and listening to Grandma Dash's stories. We had no idea of the trauma to come.

"See, you young people, you have to learn everything you can. Just git out there and take it all in. Math and Spanish and Rooshian and doctoring and such. Then you won't be thick like me."

"Grandma," Hatty comforted her, "You're not thick."

"I am. Herbert always said I was thick as a concrete slab."

"But you know embroidery and cooking and stuff."

"But nothing on paper. What you got on paper young Red?"

She asked me this in the middle of a tentative bite of bagel, and I almost choked.

"Well, I'm going to major in psychology."

"What? You going biking?"

Hatty realised what she meant. "No, Grandma, he's not cycling, he's studying the mind."

"Whose mind? Ain't nobody kin unnerstan the humin mind. In particular, my Herbert's. He was part Lithuanian, which meant he was miserable down to the long-johns and ass cheeks. Even the well-covered bits were downright depressed. The bits you saw was glum, but the dark bits was something shocking and he narrowly missed being put away."

We were saved from further trials when the tragedy unfolded. There was the old Dodge, being driven erratically, and it was followed by Two Winds screaming like a maniac. We couldn't quite make it out but it sounded like, "Git my bag!"

All became clear when the truck pulled up and Oswald strode across to take hold of an ice-cream.

"Geez, Grandma Dash, you're great!"

He was oblivious of the three of us staring in stunned silence at the truck behind. He had reversed, and there in the back was a heap of road-kill among the paper and tin: a few dead rabbits, a cat, a black bird and the back-end of a coyote.

But on top, arms spread out wide and eyes glaring at the blue sky was Siggy.

Two Winds panted into sight. "Git my bag on the front seat, quick!"

Hatty raced for the bag. Two Winds sat down squat and fought for breath.

"Oswald Watter, what did you do?" Grandma Dash asked, like a head mistress.

"I drove the truck," he beamed.

"You idiot! I mean what did you do to Mr. Hortmann?"

"Oh, he died. I lifted him up with the rest of the road-kill. He was heavier 'n a big dog." He carried on licking the ice-cream. "And you recall, a slow wind tells you a heat-wave comes."

Hatty, Two Winds and me sprinted to the body of Siggy and felt for a pulse, put a mirror to his mouth, patted his cheeks and all the rest.

Finally, Two Winds tried his Elixir of the Crow Nation and mumbled something about the Great Spirit, then pronounced Siggy dead and that "his spirit is crossing the rainbow."

It was all sorted out official. He had not been hit by a rogue vehicle. Oswald said the old man just fell like a cut sapling in the middle of barking out an order. His legs jumped a bit, then he gargled and went still.

But I have to say, with hand on heart, that the day put a kick into my life. Hatty, real beautiful, cuddled up and did some weeping, some serious jerking and sobbing and stuff, even so my tee-shirt was wet. The drive home was weird. I mean, we never thought to cover him with a blanket, so the truck jolted to a halt by the gas station and folk walked out of the Corner Mart to stare at the sight.

The law had questions, but the man was living on borrowed time anyway, his friends said. Someone said he was the last of the Hortmanns, and they had been here since way back, but everybody had forgotten. At the funeral service, the old timers spent hours trying to recall the names of his eight brothers, all long dead.

Two Winds said he thought Siggy had a cousin a few miles west in Alzheimer, a place notorious for its green town sign: *Welcome to Alzheimer. Pop. ??*

Me? I went to Lincoln and I studied psychology. Hatty came with me and did a special project on whatever disease Oswald Watter was supposed to have. Grandma Dash said he was just thick, and that it was caused by the heat and the Bosh-Bosh fly that bit your genitals.

We stopped adopting the highway after that, leaving nature to take its course. There's been a noticeable increase in buzzards since that fateful day. Chet Two Winds left, but is supposed to be still alive, dancing in a Wild West show at the age of 130 (but them's Cheyenne years).

Chet Two Winds wrote about all this road-kill and Hortmann stuff, and gave me it to ask my opinion. This is it. He sat on an old log, alive with termites, and he talked about the dead man:

'This is a story I heard from the old ones, and it was told to me in another form, but I also was actually there when it happened. Yes, the day we lost Siggy Hortmann, like we lost so much else in that place. I've moved west since then, but that time was typical of the way the White Eyes have shat on all the good things that the Great Spirit gave us.

I mean, take burgers. By all that's holy, what is a burger? It's a great crumbled chunk of cow's ass knocked together again by a crockhead in a red overall and then served to you covered in dry leaves so you don't see the spewy mess underneath.

Still, that is not the story I heard from the old ones. The story of how the old schoolmaster died that day in Nebraska.'

He went on and on about that day on the highway, but me - well, I had that kiss from Hatty and that's all I really want to remember. But Siggy, in his death, was what brought us together. Yes, the teacher-man had a magical touch when it came to romance. Hetty and I found a peaceful spot out in the sun, underneath the walkway where the beer-barrels are rolled, and we could hear every word Chet said. He was telling his tale, thinking we were listening. But I took her in my arms and I could see that she still had tears welling up in her sweet eyes, with their dark-green that comes, I was told, from her Irish ancestry. I wiped away the tears with my bandanna. Then I touched one of her eye-lids gently with my lips.

'You're, you're not a kid anymore are you Jared?' She said, whispering.

Close by, Chet went on:

'Siggy Hortmann was not an intellectual, though many said he was. This was based on his aimless ramblings about the so-called classics of our literature. He was a man burned up with envy, as I know after one night spent with him drinking too much beer. He opened a drawer in his desk and showed me several thousand sheets of paper with typing on.

"My great novel," he said, tears welling up in his weary old eyes, "Rejected by every fiction publisher from New Orleans to Seattle and you know why? Could you care to hazard a guess, as I know you're a literary man?"

Now I wasn't a literary man. I once wrote a haiku for him and he read it in class. But I simply said, "No idea."

"My friend because it's in High German."

Now I tried to be helpful so I asked why couldn't he take it down a peg or two and put it in Lower German and then maybe the publishers would understand it. He gave me a look like my grandfather used to say Bill Hickok gave him when he asked the white man what a poker game was.

'We was like blood brothers, Siggy and me and the day we lost him was real heavy. Problem being, I was too damn old and slow to get to him. I knew he was on his way out. I get like this shiver below the gut, across the pelvis, whenever some poor soul is crossing the rainbow and I felt it then. You listening, Jared?'

"Oh sure... carry on Chet" I said, trying not to snigger. But Hatty was chuckling to herself. Chet meandered on.

'I was just rootling around for some jabjab berries on account of my bladder trouble, when the cretin comes past a-driving of the Dodge. I mean, he was smiling and there in the back, his arms jerking out their last spasms, was my old bookish amigo, Siggy. My wattly old flesh and my flat feet let me down. I sensed him ebbing away.'

Hatty had to put her hand over my mouth to stop me laughing now. Oh that sweet hand! It was turning out to be one of them days that get imprinted on you like a brand on a steer.

'Course I've always been unlucky. I was born with a crooked leg and a bad, moody star above. My mother went into a decline as soon as she saw me, fading away in a week or so, then I was brought up by an Irishman looking for the crock of gold over the rainbow in Oregon, left to perish on the slopes of some snow-line ridge, then found by a bear and rescued from his clutches by a hillbilly named Sam Britches. That was before I was adopted by the Cheyenne, and a Cheyenne I am deep

down and to this day I'm blessed with the vision of seeing into people's souls thanks to my teacher, Squint-Eyes. And if you kin follow that you're a top-drawer miracle guy who should be a Harvard Prof.'

Chet, now sitting on the rotting steps of the old barn, still rambled on about Siggy:

'I digress. You want to know about that day. Well, truth is, he tried to lift the back-end of a deer all by hisself and his gut ripped. I know, I saw it in a dream a month before. When that half-wit skidded past in the wagon, I knowed it was the bust gut. The position of the splayed arms gave that away to tell true.

'I miss him bad. No other sucker tends to listen to my tales anyway. That's why I headed west and took up dancing for the tourists. I tend to get introduced by the MC from North Platte as Old Two Winds, 140 years old (Cheyenne years) doing a dance of death, in which I trundle about muttering the names of all the U.S. presidents for ten minutes, then rattle a bull's scrotum, roll in the earth, and take the applause. Problem is, you live in sheer dread of some know-all swot who actually does know a parcel about the Cheyenne and asks a tough question or barracks you from the back of the crowd.

Poor Siggy, I miss him bad. As to that black day, well, I recall the young couple kissing and cuddling, and that can't be all bad. And of course that mad old body Dash something. Never could take her brand of abuse. She couldn't make cherry pie and her lemonade was like possum-piss.

And I know, cos I DRUNK possum-piss, but that's another story, and I wouldn't tell you anything so unhealthy in the same breath as lamenting the passing of poor Siggy. Up across the rainbow, he'll be boring the pants off the angels –

110

particularly as they should be conversant with High German, being so damned smart.'

It was no use. A man could not concentrate on learning about love under such circumstances. Hatty and I moved on, and forever, after that fateful day, references to possum-piss would be romantic, because if ever I wanted to cheer her up, I'd just mention to Hatty that there was coffee, coke or possum-piss and she would choke up and laugh fit to expire through lack of breath.

THE WALL

Glenda Young

"Mama!" she heard the boy cry. "Mama!"

But she had nothing to give. The last of the food had now gone. All she could do was give of herself and softly she started to sing. She pushed her face to the wall and the cold, hard brick scratched her cheek and her nose. The sounds from within her rose and fell as she cried into the wall. She could only hope that the boy could hear his mama as clearly as she had heard her son. Brick dust fell into her mouth as she sang, her lips scraping the wall with every note that left her mouth. Her breaths were returned to her, the wall didn't want them, and she felt the warmth of her breathing spread back to her face.

When they still had food, she would throw it over the wall for Tomas, to quieten him. The food would stifle his hunger and her pain. She kept him alive; that was all she could do. Fruit from the trees that had once hung lush with juice in the orchard was all eaten, all gone. They have been left to starve and to die. She could have run to the free world, far away from the wall. But she would never leave Tomas who was on the other side. While he cried, she knew he was alive.

The wall went up quickly. One day soldiers arrived, laughing. Lorries and trucks filled with stones roared into their village. A hole was dug, a long hole, a trench and more holes. Metal posts were knocked into the ground, like stakes through her heart. At first, it was exciting, an attraction, and the villagers came to watch, some even to help.

Tomas laughed with the soldiers, one of them played football with him, using a small stone as a ball. Then one day after playing football the soldier told Maya what was really going on. "A wall was being built", he said. "A wall to keep out the bad guys, to keep in the good. A wall to let the world know who is who," the soldier said. "And who is not?" she replied. He couldn't look at her eyes, but she saw deep into his.

After the soldiers and trucks disappeared, stones and rocks piled up around their homes. Many of Maya's friends walked to the free world, afraid of being caught on the wrong side of the wall. Come with us, they begged her, but she had the orchard and Tomas to care for, and knew of no other life.

Those from the North were paid to build, brick by brick. She knew of the Northerns, knew how they were stubborn and strong, built to work and to slave. They didn't speak her tongue and she offered her language to them in the lemons from her trees. They sucked fruit as they worked under a hot sun they were not used to. When they took a break from their work, they sat in the shade of the wall they had built, spitting pips from the citrus she had plucked from her trees. They called her crude names, shouted obscenities to her and to Tomas. They thought she did not understand but she did, she knew. And in return she offered bad fruit, with maggots inside; it was the only weapon she had.

The Northerns laid out two, three rows of bricks that stretched into the distance as far as she could see, to her left and to her right. The next day another four, five rows of bricks appeared on top. It grew higher, always higher, two rows at a time. She and Tomas stayed on the free world side of the wall. By then she was the only one left from her village. Travellers seeking refuge in the free world would stop, drawn to the orchard for shade and refreshment which she would provide. Come with us, they begged, but she shook her head, slowly. "Where would I go?" she replied, but they had no answer to give.

At night she cradled Tomas under her favourite pomegranate tree, opening up the fallen brown fruit to reveal its ruby jewels inside. She sang to Tomas, as she had always sung to Tomas, but now her voice was quiet and soft, her words muted, her lips barely moving, so that the Northerns did not hear. In the evenings, they slept in their tents and their vans, in the huts from which the villagers had fled. They cooked on stoves above which the sweet smell of ox flesh drifted on the air and pulled at Maya's stomach.

One day when the wall was six, seven bricks high Tomas disappeared. The Northerns listened to her screams as she demanded her son back. They did not understand her words but they knew what had happened, and did not care. She found him, hours later, on the other side of the wall, he was eating an orange, stuffing it into his mouth as juice ran down his fat face. Maya reached over the bricks and pulled her son to her chest. But Tomas disappeared again, some days later.

She searched first for him this time before approaching the Northerns. They shook their head, 'no. no'. In return she cut lemons in half and pissed on them before handing them over as they sat in the shade of their work.

"Mama!" she heard him cry one day. "Mama!" and she knew, she just knew, where he was. She tore up fruit and threw mouth sized pieces over the wall. And when he cried, she took his pacifier from her breast pocket and threw that to him too. She tore down tree branches and threw them over the wall which was now fourteen, fifteen bricks high. Some of the branches bounced back to her; she had not the energy or the power to give her son what he needed, not even shade from the sun.

The soldiers returned and the one with the smile came to see her. He put his hand to the air around his left knee, where Tomas' head might have reached, and his shoulders shrugged a question. Maya pointed to the wall and the smile left the soldier's face. He looked behind him, twice, before he brought out tools from his kit bag and chiselled a hole. It was the tiniest hole, but it was enough for Maya, just enough to see Tomas again.

"Tomas!" Maya cried. She put her lips to the space and kissed it. Tomas's finger wiggled into her mouth and she laughed. The soldier looked behind him again and walked off.

Maya pushed a finger into the hole to reach Tomas, but the hole was too small. She tried again with the little finger on her right hand, and this time the hole accepted. She and Tomas on their sides of the wall, finger tips touching. She chewed up leaves and what was left of the fruit and fed Tomas from her tongue, pressing her mouth hard to the wall. "Mama!" he would cry. "Mama!"

Maya knew that while there was a cry she would never leave the wall.

And softly she started to sing.